# THE FIFTH ELEMENT™

Voyager

A NOVEL BY
**TERRY BISSON**

FROM THE SCREENPLAY BY
**LUC BESSON & ROBERT MARK KAMEN**

BASED ON A STORY BY
**LUC BESSON**

# THE FIFTH ELEMENT™

A FILM BY LUC BESSON

HarperCollins*Publishers*

*Voyager*
An Imprint of HarperCollins*Publishers*
77–85 Fulham Palace Road,
Hammersmith, London W6 8JB

A Paperback Original 1997
1 3 5 7 9 8 6 4 2

*The Fifth Element* © Gaumont 1997

*The Fifth Element*™ /

© Pocket, 1997 for the novelization

A catalogue record for this book
is available from the British Library

ISBN 0 00 648346 1

Cover artwork © Guild Pathe Cinema Ltd

First printing: May 1997

Printed and bound in Great Britain by
Caledonian International Book Manufacturing Ltd, Glasgow

Visit Gaumont on the World Wide Web at http://www.gaumont.com

# 1

It was 1913 and "The War to End All Wars," World War I, had not yet begun.

Other wars were raging, though.

The War of the Desert Against the Nile was continuing its eons-old pitched battle here at the desert's edge where the village fields met the dunes; the battle yielding up a little more sand one year, a little more cultivated ground the next.

The War of Animal Against Man was being fought out by a mule with a boy on its back, slowly plodding along a track leading into the desert, away from the village fields. The mule went slower and slower, until the boy hit him with a stick between the ears, gaining a temporary advantage in the war.

"Go," said Omar in a native dialect as ancient as the tombs that dotted the landscape. "But not too fast," he added.

The boy was fighting his own war—the eternal War of Youth Against Age. He had been sent to fetch water, and he was in no hurry to get back so that the grown-ups could boss him around some more.

Meanwhile other, deeper wars were gathering, wars of which boys and mules knew not.

The track wound between the dunes, into the desert. The sun burned down on scattered ruins. None of them had names.

Over the years the ancient tombs and temples came and went, like clouds, uncovered and then covered again by the shifting sands. It sometimes seemed to Omar that it was the ruins that moved and not the dunes; for indeed, the eternal desert seemed far more substantial than the tombs and temples that appeared and disappeared at the whim of the elements.

Omar passed the professor's Model T, buried in sand up to the tops of its wheels. Later today his uncle would come with a camel to pull it out. For a price.

Omar and his mule plodded along the bottom of the wadi, and up the rise that led to the new tomb. Even from a distance it was impressive.

It was one Omar hadn't seen before. His uncle had told him that it had appeared several times in the past, but had been ignored by the grave robbers, since it held no treasure.

"It is not for us," he said.

Omar's uncle was a tomb robber. The locals

robbed tombs and temples for greed. The Europeans came and robbed them for something called science.

The Europeans intrigued Omar. They were more like boys than men. They were as cruel as boys, but as quick to laugh. Like boys, they didn't seem to care for gold or silver. The Italian professor was as excited by the graffiti he had found as a "real" robber would have been by circles of gold or baskets of precious stones.

Even half buried in the sand, the temple was impressive. Its huge pillared entrance dwarfed the two boys who stood on the sand outside, holding mirrors to reflect light into the temple (a grave robber's trick).

The boys waved at Omar as he passed. "Water!" they cried, and Omar stopped to share a few drops from the goatskin bags.

"You're not thirsty!" he said. "Just bored. Be thankful you've got a job."

"Quit playing the sahib," said Mahmoud, who held the largest mirror. "You're just a water boy."

Omar decided to ignore him.

He left the mule in the shade and hurried inside. Omar knew that the professor and his American helper, Billy, would be thirsty. The Europeans drank a lot of water.

The mirrors at the door shone down a long corridor. Omar walked close to the wall so that he wouldn't block the light.

Another boy held another mirror at the end. His job was to direct the beam inside, and make sure the light followed the professor and his young American around the big chamber.

But the boy was already messing up. His head dropped as he dozed off, made drowsy by the dim light, the bad air, or perhaps by the droning of the Italian archeologist as he explained the hieroglyphics that covered the far wall of the great chamber.

"Hey, Aziz!"

The professor's voice resounded through the chamber.

The boy sat up, his light flashing around the inside of the chamber like silver lightning.

"You must pay attention!" said Professor Pacoli.

"Yeah, Aziz!" Omar whispered. He paused in the doorway, savoring the last moment of freedom before the grown-ups saw him. He was enchanted by the sight of the chamber with its far wall covered with scratchings. In the darkness they looked like graffiti; yet when the light struck them they seemed to glow with magic, with promise, with power.

The professor stood on a rickety ladder pointing out the ideographs, while the young American, Billy, drew them in his sketchbook.

Omar liked Billy. He liked to watch him work. Billy drew without even looking down at the sketchbook in his hand, and yet, his drawings were almost as perfect as the new "photographs" Omar had seen in a "magazine" from Cairo.

Omar figured the scientists (who loved the new) would have used photographs, but the light was too dim in the temple.

Omar picked up his goatskins again, and started to cross the room when he felt a bony hand on his shoulder.

He started and jumped—then looked back and saw a slight, stooped familiar figure.

Omar knew the old priest. He had been around for years, living at the edge of the desert. He wasn't quite European, but not quite Egyptian either.

The priest gently lifted the goatskin bag off Omar's shoulder.

"I will take it to them, my son."

Omar nodded and handed over the water bag. The old priest made him nervous, though he didn't know why.

"Go with God," said the priest, making the sign of the cross on the boy's forehead.

He left him in the shadows and crossed with the goatskin, toward the ladder where the Italian was going through the script, character by character:

". . . when the three planets are in eclipse," the professor said, his fingers traveling lightly across the strange characters, almost as if he were reading braille. "The black hole, like a door, is open. Evil comes . . . sowing terror and chaos!"

He reached up and pointed to an ideograph of a snake slithering between three planets. The ladder rocked and almost fell.

"See, Billy?" he said to the young man with the sketchbook. "The snake, Billy. Make sure you get the snake! The Ultimate Evil. Make *sure* you get the snake!"

Billy sketched without looking down, his hand swift and his strokes sure.

"And just when is this snake act supposed to occur?" he asked dryly.

The professor ignored his sarcasm. He turned back toward the wall and ran his fingers along the script.

"If this is the five, and this is the thousand . . . every five thousand years!"

"So we have time," Billy said.


The old priest paused, halfway across the chamber. He winced when he heard the sarcasm in the young American's voice.

*If only he knew!* For a moment, the priest wavered in what he was about to do. The young man was ignorant, after all. And ignorance was a kind of innocence. He knew nothing.

Then the old priest heard the professor's words, droning on as he followed the script:

"So here we have these different peoples or symbols of people, gathering together these four elements of life: water, fire, earth, air . . ."

The professor's fingers paused on the one ideogram that had a human shape.

"Around a fifth one, a Fifth Element."

And the priest knew that he had to do what he was about to do.

He pulled the ancient vial out of the pocket of his rough black cassock. He opened it, and winced at the sharp smell that emerged from the dry powder.

He opened the goatskin water bag as the professor droned on:

"It's like all these people gave something from themselves to make this *being* . . ."

"Lord forgive me," whispered the priest as he shook the powder from the vial into the waterbag. "They already know too much. Far, far too much!"

The professor was still talking excitedly, his fingers paused on the ideograph.

". . . this *being* in which all the history of the Universe resides. All the strength, all the hope . . . to protect us from Evil . . ."

"Amen," said the old priest, filling a tin cup from the goatskin.

The professor looked down from the ladder and noticed him for the first time.

"Father!" he said. "It's the most extraordinary thing! The greatest find in history! I mean, look . . ."

The priest nodded gravely.

Excited by his own words, the professor dropped his voice, and slowed his speech to the cadence of a prayer: "Here the Good, here the Evil, and here—"

He pointed to the symbols of the four elements, arrayed around the central figure.

"A weapon against Evil! Amazing! I am going to be famous!"

"Then let us toast your fame!" the priest said. "Here Billy . . ." He handed the young artist the cup, and poured another for the professor.

Billy began to drink as the professor climbed down the ladder.

"Drink!" said the priest, handing the professor the other cup.

The professor raised it. "To fame! Salud . . ."

But then—

He lowered the cup without tasting it.

"We cannot toast with water. Billy! In my knapsack—the grappa!"

The priest watched, horrified, as the professor threw his water onto the floor of the temple. Billy drained his cup and ran off into the corridor.

*A fitting beginning*, thought the priest, disconsolate. *I have killed the innocent one!*


*Not bad*, thought Billy. Usually the water from the goatskin tasted too much of, well, of goat, to please his palate.

But this was sweeter.

Perhaps the waterboy, Omar, had drawn it from

a better well. Or perhaps this goatskin was less foul than usual.

*Whatever*, Billy thought, as he scurried through the long corridor that led out toward the brilliant light of the desert sun. He shielded his eyes to avoid the mirrors' glare.

Halfway down the corridor, he found the professor's bag. He was bending down to open it when he heard a muffled sound, and the light changed.

Something was happening outside the temple. A sudden storm? *Impossible*, Billy thought. There were no sudden storms here. Egypt was not like Indiana, where a thunderstorm could blow up and blow over in minutes.

Here the heat was relentless, and the few clouds that appeared stayed high, as if fearing that if they came too low the people would pluck them from the sky and squeeze out whatever little moisture they held.

Billy was feeling dizzy. Was that lightning? Was that thunder? The muffled sounds were getting louder.

Billy unzipped the bag and found the machine gun the consulate had asked the professor to carry. The professor, who hated guns, had loaded it but left it in the bag.

It was a Sten—the latest model.

Underneath the Sten gun was the grappa. The bottle had lost over an inch and a half since morning. Billy had often suspected the professor used it to "facilitate" his translations of the hieroglyphics.

*Doesn't matter to me*, thought Billy. He would be back home in Indiana in a few months, unless—

But why was he feeling so dizzy?

The entrance to the temple was darkened now, and the "thunder" grew louder and louder.

Then stopped.

Billy crept closer to the door. The boys who had been holding the mirrors were staring up, dumbfounded.

Billy looked up and saw an immense metal ship, sitting on its end.

A doorway in the side of the ship was opening.

What came out was—not human.

"This perfect person," the professor read. "This perfect being . . ."

He turned toward the old priest, who stood with his eyes closed and his fingertips touching, arched in an image of a steeple.

"I know this is the key," the professor said. "But I do not understand it. *Perfect*?"

"Perfect means perfect," offered the priest.

The boys ran off into the dunes, screaming.

Billy ran back into the shadows of the temple. He didn't know what he was running for—his life, his sanity, or his sketchpad, which he had set down by the professor's bag.

He was bending over to pick it up when he heard footsteps behind him in the corridor.

Whatever they were, they were coming in!

Pressing against the wall, Billy hid in the shadows as a line of huge figures moved swiftly past. They seemed to be moving slowly, yet they passed in an instant, as if they occupied a different Time.

Arrayed in glowing metallic armor, they were as massive as eight-foot turtles walking upright, though they moved with surprising speed and grace. They seemed headless—until Billy saw the small, bird-like heads that grew from the centers of their massive chests.

Billy reached into the professor's bag. His fingertips were tingling. He was dizzy.

Could it be that all this was a nightmare?

The dream turned to cold reality as his fingers closed on the steel of the Sten.


"And this divine light the hieroglyphics talk about," the professor said. "What is *divine light*?"

At that moment, as if on cue, the chamber fell dark. A vast rumbling filled the air. The walls of the temple shook.

"Aziz!" called out the professor, without turning. "Light!"

Suddenly the chamber was filled with light.

"Much better!" said the professor, from his ladder. "Thank you, Aziz."

---

11

The professor continued to read the markings on the wall. The light was stronger than ever, revealing even more subtlety in the inscription.

"Father, this is the most unbelievable thing I have ever seen," said the professor. "Don't you . . ."

The professor turned and saw why the priest wasn't answering. He was kneeling in front of a large *thing* that looked almost like a man.

Almost, but not quite.

It was eight feet tall and as massive as a grizzly—in armor.

". . . think?" the professor finished, as two strong hands (well, almost hands) grabbed him under his arms and lifted him off the ladder.

"Are you German?" demanded the professor, his legs kicking futilely in the air.

No answer.

"*Sprechen sie Deutsch?*" the professor gasped.

No answer.

*Where was Billy?* Panicked, the professor looked around. A dozen more *things* stood around the walls, holding glowing globes that lighted the chamber.

The old priest was lying flat on the floor. The professor had always figured he was Christian—Coptic, maybe, or one of those weird desert sects.

But he seemed to be worshipping the leader of the *things*, who was standing over him. He was *talking* to it . . .

☼   ☼   ☼

"Lord," said the priest. "He was about to discover everything. But I had the situation under control."

He lay on the cold stone floor, looking up at the Mondoshawan commander.

The Mondoshawan held out his hand and helped the old priest to his feet.

His voice was deep but surprisingly gentle.

"Servant," he said, "you and the thousand guards before you have done your work well. But war is coming."

"War?" The priest shivered.

A tiny distant nod.

"We must keep them safe . . ."

"Keep who safe? Keep what safe?" asked the professor, trying unsuccessfully to keep his voice from squeaking.

It was surprising how little dignity one had when one's feet couldn't touch the floor.

The *thing* leader didn't answer. Instead it walked to the wall covered with hieroglyphics, and slid its hand along the smooth surface as if looking for an opening.

An opening that was not—could not—be there.

But there it was.

"Unbelievable!" breathed the professor as the *thing* slid a metallic finger into the opening. The wall groaned and slid open, with a grating sound of stone on sand.

The two *things* set the professor down. While

he was still struggling to find his balance, their leader stepped through the door and motioned for the rest to come with him.

The old priest hesitated for a moment, then followed them through the door.

The professor was just about to follow when one of the *things* that had stayed behind waved its great metallic hand over his head.

Gently, like a prayer or a spell.

And he slumped to the floor, unconscious.

The old priest had never been in this inner room before.

It was made of a different material from the heavy, reddish stone that formed the outer chamber of the temple.

The walls were smooth and bright, like luminous marble. They rose to form a steep pyramid, with four sides.

In each corner of the room was a rectangular, twelve-inch stone. Each stone glowed with a different color: red, green, blue and yellow.

In the center of the room was a luminous sarcophagus, resting on a low altar.

The Mondoshawan leader stopped at the altar and gazed down at the sarcophagus reverently, as if to confirm that even the gods have gods.

The old priest stood at his side.

"The Fifth Element," whispered the priest, his words as soft as a prayer.

The Mondoshawan leader nodded, showing what might have been a smile.

He took a case from one of his followers—a simple metal briefcase made out of what seemed to be aluminum, except that it looked warm.

He opened the case and held it out.

Four Mondoshawans went to the four corners of the room, and brought their leader the four glowing stones, one by one.

The stones fit into the case perfectly.

"Kommander—"

The leader closed the case and looked at the priest wordlessly.

"If you take the weapon, we will be defenseless if the Evil returns," said the priest.

The Mondoshawan nodded. "If Evil returns, so will we."

The priest nodded and lowered his eyes.

"Hands up!"

The voice came from the doorway.

The old priest turned and saw the professor's young assistant, Billy. The artist. But instead of holding a sketchpad and pencil, he was brandishing an evil-looking weapon.

"Nobody move!" Billy said.

He staggered into the room as if drunk. Only the old priest knew that he was reeling from the effects of the poison in his water.

---

"Nobody move!" Billy shouted. "I'm warning you. I have a gun. And I know how to use it. Let the priest go!"

*He thinks he's saving me*, the priest thought, amazed. *And it is I who doomed him!*

He ran across the room toward the young man.

"No, my son!" he shouted. "The Mondosha-wans are our friends. They come in peace. Put the gun down!"

"Friends!?" said Billy. He pointed behind him, to the professor's body on the floor of the outer chamber. "They killed the professor. They're monsters!"

"No, Billy."

The priest slowed to a walk. The young man was swaying from side to side. The gun was waving dangerously.

The priest held out his hand.

"Trust me!" he said in his most authoritative voice. "Put the gun down!"

But the old priest's slow movements seemed to terrify rather than reassure Billy.

He backed up: "No. You're one of them! You're . . ."

He tripped, stumbled, fell—and as he fell the Sten gun clutched in his hands sprayed the ceiling and the walls of the inner room with a wild rain of bullets:

*Bratabratabratabrat*!

"No!" shouted the priest. "Don't!"

*Bratabratabratabrat!*

---

16

Stinging sprays of rock and sand, thrown up by the bullets, stung the old priest's cheeks. Behind him, he saw the Mondashawan leader take a bullet and fall. The others closed in around him.

Billy fell backward through the door, into the outer chamber. His head hit the stone floor with a *crack*.


It was over almost as soon as it had begun. Billy lay on the floor of the outer chamber, unconscious.

The priest made the sign of the cross, then looked up.

The door was closing.

"Hurry!" the priest said. He ran to the side of the Mondoshawan leader, who had taken several hits from the Sten gun. Although there was no blood, the priest could hear the slow hissing as the alien's vital gases sublimated into the dry desert air.

The priest tried to pull the Mondoshawan leader to his feet, but it was like trying to move a piano.

The leader handed the metal case to one of his followers. Another was already carrying the sarcophagus from the altar out through the closing door.

"Hurry!" the priest repeated.

The Mondoshawan leader shook his tiny head, slowly and yet firmly.

"Servant," he said, "here is your mission now.

Keep the temple ready. Pass on the knowledge as it was passed to you."

"I will do as you command," the priest answered. "But please hurry! You still have time."

The Mondoshawan rose off the stone floor, and pushed the priest through the rapidly closing door. "Time is of no importance," he said. "Only life is important."

"But . . ."

The door closed on the Mondoshawan leader's hand. The finger that was also a key snapped off. It rang like a bell when it hit the floor at the priest's feet.

The mule was braying frantically, terrified.

Omar tried to quiet him, then backed up to get a better look at the gigantic ship. It was three times longer than any of the ships of the Europeans, and it stood straight up on the sand.

Then with a roar, it was gone. Very slowly . . . and yet all at once.

Dazed, Omar followed Aziz into the temple. The corridor was dark. The door that had opened was closed, and the chamber was as it had been.

The mirror still lay where Aziz had dropped it, reflecting the light from the setting sun.

One of the Mondoshawans' globes was in the corner, its light slowly fading. It popped like a soap bubble, and was gone.

The professor was crumpled on the floor, snoring noisily.

Billy looked dead, but he was breathing, too.

The old priest was kneeling in front of the scratchings on the wall. His hands were held upward in prayer—or triumph, maybe. Or despair.

He held up a crooked metallic finger. Or maybe it was a key.

"I will be ready, my lord," he said. "If the Evil returns."

He pointed toward three suns on the sandstone wall.

# 2

EXACTLY FIVE HUNDRED YEARS LATER, THE SAME THREE SUNS glowed on the digital control screen of a United Federation starship.

The coordinates projected from them, plotted by the fuzzilogical implicator imbedded in the EPROM chips of the starship's calculators, crossed at one point in the emptiness called space.

A captain, wearing the colorful uniform of the United Federation Space Command, stood on the bridge, studying the crossed lines with a worried air. The control screen was his only view out of the ship, since the windows of the bridge were opaqued by a protective energy shield.

A door slid open and shut behind him.

Moving buoyantly in the temporary gravity, General Staedert of the UF Central Command entered the bridge.

The arrogance and impatience of headquarters military brass was apparent in the tone of his query. "Anything yet?"

"No, sir," the captain said. The resentment of line officers to headquarters interference could be heard in the tone of his reply.

"Not even a temperature?" The general had been debriefed by his analysts earlier that morning, and he hoped his question reflected both the depth of his concern and the breadth of his knowledge.

The captain shook his head. "Our thermo-analyzers have jammed. One of them reads over a million degrees, and the other's at minus five thousand."

Staedert turned to the grizzled old man with one runny eye who had been his representative on the bridge in his absence. "Major Gruber?"

"Never seen anything like it," Gruber said, or rather, growled.

A technician on a nearby terminal broke in: "It's taking shape!"

"Let's see it," said Staedert.

"Shield," ordered the captain.

A tech slid a fingertip along a control strip. The stars appeared, one by one, as the shield powered down.

The captain and the others on the bridge were looking out on an unmapped sector of the galaxy. And in the center of it . . .

An amoebic, moving mass, swirling like a storm.

Something between a planet, an embryonic star, and a black hole.

Its writhing shape, continually changing,

evoked every horror in the universe. It altered color as it roiled and bubbled, spattered and burbled, sputtered and burned—a hideous amalgam of decaying rose, rancid green, cold blue, blood red, and gangrenous purple.

It was all the colors of death, come to life.

The captain had expected it. In fact, it was he who had reported the new disturbance in the sector. Yet even he was terrified and awestruck at the grotesque sight before him.

"What the hell can it be?" he asked.

"Send out a probe," said Staedert, in a voice that was clearly accustomed to being obeyed.

Light years away, high in the web of towers that was the office of the President of the United Federation, a rustling was heard.

The unmistakable sound of power.

The President entered. He embodied the authority of his office. He was a huge, black, burly man, of African ancestry, with the bull neck of a fullback and the steely eye of a hunter. A war hero, he had been elected in a time of peace, out of public nostalgia for the lost simplicities of interstellar conflict. But now a new conflict had arrived, even though no one knew what it was, from whence it came, or what—if anything—it meant.

"On air with Staedert in thirty seconds," whispered an aide.

The President nodded and sat down at his massive desk. His office was crowded with uniformed military men, scientists, aides, techs and advisers.

In the midst of them, all but unnoticed, was an old priest in a rough black cassock, attended by a young novice.

The young man whispered in the priest's ear, "I'll find a seat for you, Father Cornelius."

"Thank you, David, my son."

A screen lit up at one end of the room, like a doorway to the far reaches of the galaxy; as indeed it was, since it showed the bridge of a distant starship, where an identical screen was opening to show the President's office.

"President on the line, sir!"

General Staedert looked at the screen, across a wilderness of light years, at the President and his guests.

"We're in position, Mr. President," he said.

The President's deep, commanding voice shook both rooms.

"I have to address the Supreme Council in ten minutes. Just the facts, General."

"There are no results from the chemical and molecular analysis as yet," said Staedert. "All the calibers are overshot. We're initiating a thermonucleatic imaging—"

The President broke in. "What you are saying is that you don't know what it is!"

Staedert seemed, if anything, relieved. "Not yet,

Sir. The only thing we know is that it just keeps getting bigger!"

A murmur rippled through the ranks in the President's office. The old priest and the young novice kept their eyes glued to the screen.

The President turned to face his staff.

"Options!" he said. It was neither a statement nor a question; it was a command.

"Wait or act," said a general, stepping forward.

The President turned back toward the screen. "Staedert. Recommendations?"

Staedert considered for only a moment before answering. "My philosophy, Mr. President, is shoot first and ask questions later. I don't like uninvited guests."

The President swiveled in his chair. He sent his next question over the heads (literally) of the military men, addressing the scientists who stood behind them.

"Gentlemen?"

The scientists shuffled and cleared their throats. The boldest of them stood on tiptoes to speak.

"I think it would be foolish to shoot at an organism that seems to be alive, without first taking the time to study it more. Besides, it has shown no signs of hostility."

There was a murmur of protest from the military men on both sides of the screen.

The President quieted them with a barely perceptible wave of his hand.

"No . . ." he agreed. "It's just getting bigger."

"So do people," said the scientist, reddening. "But that's no reason to shoot them!"

The President seemed exasperated by this reply. "The security of the Federated territories is, and remains, number one priority," his voice boomed.

Then he lowered his voice to address his gathered generals once more.

"I suppose General Staedert's 'philosophy' is acceptable to you?"

As one, they all nodded.

The President wheeled in his chair. "All right then. Staedert?"

Suddenly a voice broke through from the back of the room. "Mr. President?"

The military men parted like the Red Sea, and a small but imposing figure moved through. It was the old priest, a short, stocky man with a strange silver amulet around his neck.

The novice followed him a respectful step behind.

"Yes?" asked the President.

"Cornelius," said the priest, stepping forward to introduce himself. "Vito Cornelius. I have a different theory to offer you, Mr. President."

The President seemed simultaneously amused and irritated by this interruption. An aide bent and whispered into his ear: "From the religious delegation, sir."

The President of the United Federation, elected guardian of 200 billion souls, both human and otherwise, studied the man who had forced himself into his circle of attention.

---

"You have twenty seconds," he said.

If his fierce look was designed to intimidate the diminutive old priest, it didn't work.

"Imagine for a moment," said Father Cornelius, "that this *thing* is not anything that can be identified, because it prefers not to be. Because it is evil. Total evil."

The President shrugged. "One more reason to shoot first, eh?"

The generals all nodded in perfect, simultaneous agreement.

Father Cornelius shook his head.

"Evil begets evil, Mr. President. Shooting would only make it stronger."

There was a flurry of activity on the screen. The President turned in his chair to watch.

"The probe will attain its objective in five seconds!" announced an excited tech on the bridge of the starship.

"Drop the shield," muttered the starship's captain, and the tech's finger slid along the control strip.

The starship's windows went clear, and for the first time the bubbling, multicolored dark mass was visible on the screen in the President's office.

A gasp went up.

Followed by a breathless silence as the blinking light of a probe drew closer and closer to its objective.

Then a groan as the probe disappeared into the

tumorous darkness—and the strange, evil mass began to boil and bubble even more furiously.

"Mr. President," cried General Staedert. "We're at a crisis point!"

"Growth rate is at twenty-seven percent!" put in a panicked technician.

All eyes in both rooms—the office and the bridge of the starship—were on the President.

Who seemed puzzled.

Without turning back toward the priest, he said politely, "Your theory is interesting, Father, but I don't think we have time to go into it right now."

"Time is of no importance," said Father Cornelius. "Only life is important."

"That's exactly what we are going to do," said the President. "Protect the lives of some 200 billion of our fellow citizens!"

He spun in his chair as if to put a period on his conversation with the priest.

"General—you may fire when ready!"


A silence fell over the room. The young novice and the old priest stood exactly where the President had left them, between his chair and the rank of sycophantic generals.

All eyes were on the screen at the far end of the office, which showed the bridge of the starship.

Staedert was giving the orders. He was all business.

"Up front loading of a 120ZR missile. Marker lights on the objective."

As he spoke, something was changing outside the starship's windows. The amoeba-like, roiling, boiling mass was taking on solid form. It was becoming a planet, covered with a null black crust.

A technician looking at a control terminal read-out confirmed what people were witnessing with their own eyes:

"Its structure has just solidified on the surface."

From the second tier of watchers in the President's office, a scientist spoke out, sending his words over the heads of the military men.

"I think it's anticipating the attack," he said excitedly. "Anticipation denotes intelligence!"

Another, quieter voice was heard—the priest's, who added: "The most terrible intelligence imaginable, Mr. President."

On hearing this, the President hesitated. But he didn't turn away from the screen. "Staedert!?"

"Yes, sir!" The general turned to face the President. He was all action, seeming to tingle from the toes of his boots to the tips of his blunt fingers.

The President looked around the room: from the generals, to the scientists, to his own aides, to the priest and the novice who stood apart, patiently watching.

"I have a doubt," said the President.

"I don't, Mr. President," muttered Staedert in reply.

And before his orders could be countermanded,

he nodded toward a tech at the starship's control board, who touched a switch—

The screen was filled with a brilliant light as the missile was fired.

The light faded to a pinprick as the 120ZR sped away, covering a thousand kilometers with a single leap, thanks to its cold-fusion faux-warp drive. It blinked briefly in and out of realspace as it zeroed in on its massive target.

Then just before impact, it shifted down from hyper to fusion drive, and with a chemical blast penetrated the evil black mass.

Following the lead of Staedert and the starship crew, the President and his entourage covered their eyes so that they wouldn't be blinded by the explosion.

Except there was no explosion.

The missile penetrated the black mass and was swallowed. There was a slight disturbance on the surface, and then—

Nothing.

But not quite nothing.

For immediately the dark planet began to grow again, at an even faster rate than before.

"Prepare to fire three," General Staedert barked. "Load a series of 240ZR missiles. Maximum shield protection."

"Yes sir," said the captain behind him.

"Staedert," said the President. "What's going on? Can you destroy it?"

"I'm about to, Mr. President."

The General gave a nod, and the tech at the control board flipped three switches.

There was a flash of light, three times as bright as before.

This time three pinpricks of light headed toward their hideous target. The missiles flickered in and out of existence as they covered the distance at a high fraction of the speed of light.

And they were absorbed as easily, as quietly, as effectively, as the first missile had been.

Except that this time, the dark planet immediately *doubled* in size!

A panicked voice came from the row of scientists in the President's office. "The planet's diameter has increased by two hundred percent!"

It was echoed by a shout from the rank of generals: "And it's moving toward the ship!"

This was enough for the President, who rolled forward in his chair and shouted at the screen. "Staedert, get out of there immediately! I don't want an incident. Do you hear me, Staedert?"

Staedert was pretending not to hear. He turned to the starship captain. "What do we have that's bigger than the 240?"

"Nothing, General."

The President, furious at being ignored, shouted: "Staedert, get out of there! That's an order!"

The volume of the President's shout triggered

the voice-activated viewscreen zoom, so that the entire screen was filled with Staedert's face.

His forehead was damp with sweat.

And something else. A thick black liquid was beading up on his brow, starting to drip down slowly, like syrup. . . .

Staedert was just about to reach up and wipe his brow, when a tremendous flash filled the screen.

The photosensitive zoom pulled back, and the screen showed the bridge of the starship again. Everyone was frozen with terror, watching a tongue of flame emerge from the black planet.

It reached toward the starship. Closer and closer.

"Good God!" Staedert cried.

And the starship was obliterated in a storm of light and noise.

"Good God!" cried the President—and behind him, in a smaller voice, the old priest whispered it more as a prayer than an exclamation—

"Good God!"

# 3

"GOOD GOD!"

Korben Dallas sat up in his bed.

There had been a blinding light, a tremendous explosion, and . . .

Korben shuddered and shook his head.

Another war nightmare.

He looked over at the clock on the bedside table. "BRRRIINNNGGG!" it said.

"Hush!" said Korben, flicking it with one finger as he reached for a cigarette.

"March 18, 2413," said the clock. "8:00 A.M."

"I know, I know," said Korben.

"Meaow" said the cat from the hall. There was a scratching sound at the door.

"I'm coming," said Korben. Then he heard the phone.

BBBBRRRRIIIIINNNNGGG!

Everything at once!

He picked up the phone as he crossed his tiny

modular apartment room toward the door, patting himself for a light.

Behind him, the bed made itself.

Korben was a well-built man in his mid-thirties, all but bald with very short hair, and good-looking in spite of the scars on his face and arms that revealed a somewhat more adventurous than judicious nature.

"Yeah?" he said into the phone. Still patting himself for a light.

"Hey, bud!" said a familiar voice. "Finger here!" His oldest friend and now his cab dispatcher.

Korben wedged open the stuck cat door and a small yellow cat ran in. "Hi, sweetie," he said.

"I love you too, Major, but you haven't called me that since basic training."

"Not you, Finger. I was talking to the cat."

Still looking for a match, Korben opened a drawer in the bedside table. It was filled with medals.

He unrolled a paper. A Medal of Honor certificate, made out to Major Korben Dallas. *For valor above and beyond the* . . .

"Oh, yeah, I forgot," said Finger. "You prefer your pet cat to the real thing."

Korben unrolled another paper. A faded photograph of himself with his ex-wife. *Beautiful, if slightly predatory* . . .

"At least the cat comes back," Korben said. He dropped the picture into the drawer and it rolled

itself back up. Under a tangle of campaign rib-
bons, he found an old fashioned book of paper
matches.

"You still pining for that two-timing slut?"
Finger asked. "Forget her. There are a million
women out there."

"I don't want a million," said Korben. He tried
a match. It didn't light. "I just want one. A perfect
one."

"Don't exist, bud."

Korben pulled out another photo. Two men in
uniform, standing in front of a batwing space
fighter. "Just found a picture of you," he said to
Finger.

"How do I look?"

Korben tried another match. It didn't light.
"Like shit."

"Must be an old one," said Finger. "Listen up—"

Korben crossed to the refrigerator and opened
it. It was bare except for a single empty container
of Gemini Croquettes. He picked it up and studied
the banner over the label: "*Win a Dream Trip for
Two to Fhloston Paradise!*"

"I'm listening," muttered Korben, closing the
refrigerator.

"You gotta bring me your hack for the six-
month overhaul," said Finger. "ASAP."

Korben crossed to the tiny sink and turned on
the tap. A dribble of brown water came out.

"Don't need an overhaul," he said.

"Sure you do."

Korben filled a pan with brackish water and put it on the stove. The burner lit automatically.

"You're forgetting who sat next to you for a thousand missions," Finger continued. "I know how you drive!"

"Finger!" Remembering his cigarette, Korben bent down to light it off the burner. "I'm driving a cab now, not a space fighter!"

"How many points you got left on your license?"

"Um . . ." Korben calculated a lie. "At least thirty."

"In your dreams. See you tonight!"

The phone clicked as Finger hung up. Korben, sighing, did the same.

The water was boiling. Korben dropped in a pill of instant Colombian. He took the saucepan off the burner and set it on the tiny three-legged table.

The burner blazed on merrily.

Korben slapped the stove.

The burner shut itself off.

"Meow." The cat jumped onto the table.

Korben set the cat's bowl on the table. He poured half the instant coffee into his own cracked cup, and half into the cat's bowl.

"Sorry, sweetie, that's all I have."

"Meaow."

Korben tapped his cup against the cat's bowl.

"Cheers."

# 4

THE OFFICE OF THE PRESIDENT OF THE UNITED FEDERATION WAS quiet. The wall screen was powered down—transparent. Beyond it, the towers of Manhattan soared into the dirty sky.

Only a few military officers remained, standing in a line in their bright uniforms, nodding in unison like soon-to-be-extinct birds.

The President was busy ignoring them.

He was bent over his massive desk, examining an ancient sketchbook. The old priest, Father Vito Cornelius, was turning the pages slowly.

"You have forty-eight hours," Cornelius said. "The time it needs to adapt itself to our living conditions."

"And then?" The President looked up, his broad dark face seamed with worry.

"And then it will be too late," said the priest. "The goal of this thing is not to fight for money or power. Its goal is to wipe out life. All forms of life!"

---

"But why?"

The diminutive old priest's eyes gazed off into space—or inward toward some dark mystery.

"I wish I knew."

Across the room, the incoming signal on the viewscreen was beeping. The screen slowly began to become opaque, obliterating the view of taxi-cabs and traffic flitting among the towers,

"So what you are telling me, Father," the President said, "is that there is nothing we can do to stop this!"

"There is only one thing."

Cornelius looked toward the screen. "And it is on its way."

Light years away, in a remote sector of the galaxy, a mile-long starship was speeding toward Earth, the home planet of the United Federation.

It was picked up and locked on by DEW (Distant Early Warning) scanners.

It was operated by a race little known to Earth, but well-known to the ancient priest, who was explaining as best he could, to the President . . .

"This is a Mondoshawan," Father Cornelius said, showing the drawing of the alien that had been made in the temple by Billy, five hundred years before.

The President studied the round, bulky body; the tiny angular head.

"The Mondoshawans have in their possession

the only weapon that can defeat the Evil that is upon is."

"Which is?"

Cornelius turned another page. "The four elements—earth, air, fire and water—gathered around a Fifth Element. The Supreme Being, the ultimate warrior, created to protect life."

The President looked skeptically at the page. It showed a human figure encased in armor. Metallic gloves held a case engraved with the emblem of the three suns.

"The case holds the Sacred Stones. Together with the Fifth Element, they produce what the ancients called the Light of Creation, able to bring life to the farthest reaches of the Universe. But if Evil stands here—"

He pointed to the Fifth Element.

"Then what?" asked the President impatiently.

Cornelius looked up, into the big man's eyes. "White turns to black. Light to dark. Life to death. For all eternity."

"Mr. President . . ."

The President turned and saw one of his generals holding a blinking cell phone.

"We have a Mondoshawan spaceship at the frontier requesting permission to enter Federation territory."

The President looked at the diminutive priest who had brought such immense news—and then at the generals. "I guess I should make a decision," he began.

"Sir!" said the general, covering the phone. "These Mondoshawans do *not* belong to the United Federation. We do not know their intentions. I recommend an immediate military interception before . . ."

The President broke in angrily.

"Did you see that *thing* swallow our starship like a gumdrop? You can't even tell me what it is! I ask you for options and you give me bullshit!"

The President slammed one massive fist down onto the desk. Father Cornelius jumped back.

"Send them my permission to enter our territory. With my warmest regards."

Cornelius let out a long sigh. "Thank you, Mr. President," he whispered, closing the ancient sketchbook he had carried with him.

# 5

PICTURE, IF YOU WILL, A SHIP AS LARGE AS A SMALL CITY, ENTER-
ing a star system to which it has been granted
access.

At the controls are the Mondoshawan elders,
those who have taken it as their sacred trust to
guard the Universe against its greatest Evil—which
manifests itself every few milennia.

The Mondoshawan are a race so serene, so
philosophical, so untroubled by small corruptions
and infelicities that their appearance, while it might
seem ungainly or even ugly to some, has a soothing
effect on all they encounter; for underneath their
rude exterior shines the demeanor of a fully
evolved race that has made peace with itself and
with the Universe.

The Mondoshawan ship reflects the grandeur
of its builders. It is large, a little ungainly, but
stately in its movements and steadfast in its pur-
poses.

But the ship is not alone. Following it, a little

above and behind, are two nasty looking warships
that look like killer jellyfish.

Mangalore warships.

Now imagine, if you will, a race of beings so ugly
that evolution has provided them with temporary
shapeshifting powers, so that they can look in the
mirror without suffering the shock of seeing themselves.

The Mangalores have developed their evasive
genius to a high art, and are using it to hide from
the Mondoshawan space ship. They are following
above and behind (behind in time as well as space,
and above in space as well as time), and closing
fast.

The Mangalore at the controls is about to experience his race's greatest joy. Total destruction. For
the Mangalore, there is no greater pleasure than to
destroy something more beautiful than itself. And
that includes everything in the Universe.

And this time he's even getting paid for it!

This is a plethora, a cornucopia of delights. He
is going to hit the Mondoshawan ship from
behind, without warning. Sneakiness is its own
reward.

He hits the controls with an almost sexual thrill
(sex among the Mangalores is intimately linked
with killing) and pulls down.

A blast.

A hit.

Confusion reigns aboard the Mondoshawan ship. For while the Mondoshawan are reconciled to their own deaths, they are fully aware of the importance of the weapon they are delivering to a defenseless Earth.

The Mangalore fires again. And again.

And again.

Another hit. This one fatal.

The Mondoshawan ship veers toward a tiny nearby planet.

The Mondoshawan commander locates an uninhabited area, and locks the controls.

The blast shakes the sky . . .

# 6

"WELCOME TO PARADISE!"

"WELCOME TO PARADISE!"

Korben Dallas paused on his way to the door.

The TV screen behind him was filled with an image of palm trees, blue water, white sand.

"Damn!" Korben cursed under his breath. He wished he could afford a TV with an OFF switch. The cheap (i.e., free) model that filled one corner of his modular apartment lighted up whenever a commercial was on. They arrived unannounced, like the mail-order catalogs of yore.

"Welcome to Fhloston Paradise! Tonight, from five to seven, Loc Rhod, the ultimate DJ, the man listened to by more people than anyone else in the Universe . . ."

The cat watched, entranced.

". . . will announce the winner of the Gemini Croquettes Contest. Two days in Fhloston Paradise!"

"Don't watch it all day," Korben said, scratching the cat between the ears. "It'll rot your mind."

The cat meowed distractedly, eyes fixed on the palm trees and blue water.

"Gemini Croquettes!" the announcer's voice droned. "The perfect meal for a perfect world!"

Korben opened his apartment door onto a less than perfect world.

A man stood in the hallway. A kid, really; maybe eighteen. Not too big.

But the laser weapon leveled in Korben's face was plenty big. And lethal. It was humming dangerously.

"The cash, man!" the kid said.

Korben restrained a laugh. *Cash? Who ever carried cash?*

"Been here long?" he asked.

"Long enough!" the kid said. "The cash—or I'll blow you into tomorrow. The cash!"

"Right. The cash." Korben studied the young highwayman's (or was it hallwayman's?) weapon. "Say, isn't that a Z140? Alleviated titanium. Neuro-charged assault model?"

The kid, who had "borrowed" the weapon from his sister's ex-boyfriend's father's next-door neighbor, studied the laser rifle. "Uh . . ."

"You know," said Korben genially, "you could hurt somebody with this puppy. Good thing it's not loaded."

The kid looked hurt. "It's not?"

"Nope. You gotta push this little yellow button."

Korben pointed to a switch on the side of the gun.

The kid pushed the button. "Thanks."

The Z140's hum died.

And Korben made his move.

With his right hand, he sent the kid to the floor of the hallway, while with his left hand, he plucked the gun from the would-be mugger's hand.

"You know," Korben said, "these things are VERY illegal."

The kid hit the floor, and looked up, dazed.

"You could get in a shitload of trouble. I better hang onto it for you."

Korben opened a drawer just inside his apartment module. It was filled with similar weapons. He jammed in the Z140 and shut the drawer—

"Excuse me!"

—then stepped over the kid on the floor as his door locked behind him.

"Please enter your license."

Korben slid a plastic card through the slot on the dashboard of "his" taxi.

He punched in the stats and codes. The turbines whined. The gyros hummed.

"Welcome.on.board.Mr.Dallas," said a robotic voice.

"How you doing this morning?" Korben asked. "Sleep OK?"

He hit a button on the dash, right under the sticker that read UN UNLEADED FUEL ONLY and the door to the garage slid open.

The gyros hummed. The turbines whined.

The cab slid forward on its mag field; or rather the mag field slid forward, and the cab stayed centered exactly within it. The effect, however, was the same.

"Fuel.level.6.03," said the cab. "Propulsion.2X4."

"I had the worst goddamn nightmare," Korben muttered. "And I don't mean the stupid mugger." He could still feel the explosion in his head.

After flying a thousand missions with Finger, he was used to talking during countdown and check-off and take off; even if it meant talking to himself. Or to a stupid taxi chip.

"You.have.five.points.left.on.your.license," the taxi chip droned.

In the old days, when points were penalties, that would have been good. Now, when your points were gone, your license was lifted.

"Thanks for reminding me," said Korben.

He hit FORWARD.

The cab slid forward, off the ramp and into the air.

The megalopolis that was twenty-sixth century New York came into view. From up here, high above the trash that settled to the ground like autumn leaves, it was breathtakingly beautiful.

"Have.a.nice.day," said the taxi chip.

"Why not?" said Korben as he skimmed off between the gleaming towers, looking for his first fare.

# 7

NOT TOO FAR AWAY, IN THE OFFICE OF THE PRESIDENT OF THE
United Federation, a desperate silence reigned.

The President sat speechless in his chair. Only
minutes before he had received the news that the
Mondoshawan ship, entering the system at his invitation, had been shot down.

Only seconds before he had summoned the
priest and given him the bad news.

They say it is better to give than to receive,
but the President had always found it better—
or at least easier—to receive bad news than to
give it.

Father Cornelius had responded to the president's words by collapsing silently in a chair.
The novice, David, crouched, stunned, at his
side.

Finally, Cornelius broke the silence. "We are
lost!" he said simply.

At that moment, the President's highest-ranking
military commander, General Munro, entered the

office with a still-warm fax. "Mr. President," he said, "the attack was launched by two unregistered warships."

"Close all borders," responded the President. "And declare a state of general alert."

"Yes, sir." General Munro saluted and left the room.

The President turned to another officer who stood behind him. "Try to contact these Mondoshawans," he said. "We owe them an explanation."

"Yes sir."

"Lost!" repeated Father Cornelius. "Five hundred years we have been waiting, and all for nothing!"

The President laid his big hand on the priest's small shoulder.

"Father, you should go home. Get some rest."

The priest looked up, his eyes swimming with tears. "But the Mondoshawans . . . I am their contact on Earth! They will come for me."

"Father," the President said sternly. "This is government business now. I will keep you informed."

He motioned to two guards, who came and helped the old man to his feet.

They escorted him out of the office, and the novice, David, followed.

The door had barely slid shut behind them before it glided open again.

A captain entered.

"Sir, the rescue team has reported from the Mondoshawan crash site."

"Any survivors?"

"Technically speaking," said the captain, "yes."

# 8

"AN ARM?"

General Munro followed the surgical cart down the hallway of the Neurological Center.

He was struggling to keep up with Dr. Mactilburgh, the white-coated scientist who was pushing the cart.

On the surgical cart was an arm, still in its long metal glove. The hand was holding a broken handle.

"That's all that survived?" Munro asked.

"A few cells are still alive," said Dr. Mactilburgh. "It's more than I need."

General Munro studied the glove with its long tapering fingers. It looked almost human. It was certainly not as gross as he had expected it to be.

"It doesn't exactly look Mondoshawan," he said. "Have you identified it?"

"We tried," said Mactilburgh, pushing the cart through one set of swinging doors, then another,

51

then another. "But the computer went off the charts."

"Charts?" asked Munro, struggling to keep up.

"You see—" explained Mactilburgh, lowering his voice but not slowing "—Normal human beings have forty DNA memo groups, which is more than enough for any species to perpetuate itself. But this . . ."

He burst through yet another door, and Munro scurried to keep up.

". . . this has *two hundred thousand* DNA memo groups!"

"Sounds like—a freak—of nature—to me!" panted Munro, out of breath.

"Yes," said Mactilburgh. He stopped in front of the last barrier, a frosted glass sliding door marked
CENTRAL LAB
NEUROLOGICAL CENTER
—and flashed the general a thin smile. "I can't wait to meet him."


The Central Lab looked more like an engine room than a laboratory. It was a place for achievements, not experiments—a monument to practical rather than visionary science.

In the center of the room, a huge glass turbine hummed softly. It was filled with a clear liquid which boiled and bubbled. Floating in the liquid was the arm, still in its metallic glove.

The fingers were curved slightly. It looked like

the last gesture of a drowning race—or the first hello of a race being born.

(Both of which it was, as Munro and Mactilburgh were about to discover.)

Mactilburgh was studying the read-out on a computer terminal. To Munro, who stood at his side, it was just a long list of numbers. To Mactilburgh it was a window into a genetic code.

A genetic code unlike any he had ever seen.

"The compositional elements of his DNA chain are the same as ours. There are simply more of them—tightly packed with infinite genetic knowledge. Almost as if this being were— engineered."

General Munro, the warrior, took the warrior's view. "Is there any danger?"

Mactilburgh, the scientist, interpreted it as a health question. "We put it through the cellular hygiene detector. The cell is, for lack of a better word, perfect."

"Okay," said Munro. He had been sent by the President to monitor this experiment, and he knew his duty.

Using the key that had been provided to him by the Academy of Military and Cultural Sciences, he opened the self-destruct box.

"Go ahead," he said. He put his finger over the flashing red button. "But Mr. Perfect had better be polite. Otherwise, I turn him into cat food."

Mactilburgh nodded and pulled the switch that began the DNA reconstruction.

As the two men watched, the liquid in the circular center generator began to swirl. It began to boil. It began to bubble.

The meter on the side of the turbine showed 7, then 8, as the turbine's hum built to a high whine, then passed out of the range of human hearing. But the steady vibration of the floor and the walls continued to increase.

"Look!" said Mactilburgh excitedly.

The meter was at 9.

Tiny specks were appearing in the swiftly moving fluid. They came seemingly out of nowhere, like snowflakes in headlights; they danced and spun like sparks from an unseen fire; they glittered and glowed like stars, forming a new universe and gathering into galaxies.

The shower of sparks flowed downward in a spiral like a galaxy; then, as the two men watched, amazed, the spiral began to form into the outline of a human body.

The meter hit 10.

What had been all light and motion began to collect into form and substance. First the white of bone, and then the red of blood and flesh wrapping itself around the bone. Veins drew themselves in, and nerves snapped into place. Sinews criss-crossed the form, pulling and tugging it into a the familiar shape of a human body.

It was like watching the opposite of decay—the composition of corporeal life.

"I had no idea the process was so—beautiful!" said Mactilburgh as he stood transfixed in front of the glass.

General Munro held back, one hand hovering over the destruct button.

The meter was bouncing off the peg at 11.

"Three seconds to ultraviolet protection," said Mactilburgh's white-coated assistant from a control station across the lab.

A semi-opaque shield dropped down inside the chamber, hiding the reconstructing body from view.

"What's happening?" asked Munro.

"This is the crucial phase," said Mactilburgh. "The cells are bombarded with slightly greasy solar atoms, which force the body to react."

"React?"

"Protect itself," said Mactilburgh. "That means growing skin! Clever, huh?"

"Wonderful," said Munro. But he kept his hand poised, just in case.

The meter began to drop.

10.

9.

The process was slowing.

Dr. Mactilburgh looked at his assistant across the lab and nodded.

The young man in the white coat spoke softly into his voice-activated terminal.

"Reconstruction complete. Engage reanimation."

There was a WHHOOOOSSHHH! of air from the turbine chamber.

Munro's hand moved back into place above the flashing red self-destruct button. One push and the lab would no longer exist.

A form was barely visible through the shield. The bubbling liquid was turning to smoke, as it sublimated from a liquid into a gas.

"Activate life-support system," said Mactilburgh.

His assistant pushed a button.

CRACKKK! CRACKKK!

Lightning strikes formed in and around the chamber, causing the few strands of hair on Mactilburgh's head to dance, like wallflowers hoping to be invited onto the floor.

"Life-support system activated," said the assistant.

A sound like giant footsteps came over the loud-speaker:

*BOOM! BOOM! BOOM!*

"The heartbeat, amplified!" said Mactilburgh, turning down the volume.

*boom pitpat boom pitpat boom*

The form inside the chamber jerked.

Once, twice.

It could barely be seen through the semi-opaque shield, but it was moving as it emerged from the darkness of non-existence, into the light of creation. It was beginning to twist and writhe (or was it a dance?) in a sinuous and graceful movement.

"He's alive!" said Mactilburgh. "Remove the shield."

The aide pushed another button, and the shield slowly rose out of the way.

The chamber was empty both of liquid and gas. Only a few wisps of smoke remained. The laboratory was filled with a smell at once sweet and strange, like the soul-satisfying scent of a far field filled with flowers.

Mactilburgh, his assistant, and General Munro all stood transfixed, watching in silent wonder.

Someone was in the chamber.

A woman; a girl, really. No more than eighteen or nineteen.

She had bright red hair and huge green eyes. She was holding the same broken handle the arm had held. It appeared to be torn off a briefcase.

Her body was perfectly formed and perfectly beautiful . . . and she was nude except for a few strategically placed strips of surgical tape.

"I told you . . . perfect!" said Mactilburgh, turning to Munro.

The General seemed hypnotized.

Mactilburgh gently pushed Munro's hand away from the flashing red self-destruct button.

Munro couldn't take his eyes off the almost nude vision inside the chamber. "I'd like to get a few pictures," he said. "For the, uh, archives."

Smiling, Mactilburgh pressed a button and a camera swiveled toward the chamber. A flash went off and the girl jumped backward, startled.

Her green eyes edged in black darted around the lab. She looked at the broken handle clutched in her fingers.

"Oucra cocha o dayodomo binay ouacra mo cocha ferji akba ligounai makta keratapla," she said. "Tokemata tokemata! Seno santonoi-aypa! Monoi ay Cheba! Givamana seno!"

"What's she saying?" asked Munro, his hand once again hovering over the self-destruct button.

Mactilburgh edged Munro's hand away. "Activate the phonic detector," he said to his assistant.

The girl was kicking the glass side of the chamber.

Mactilburgh's assistant rolled out a speaker assembly festooned with more lights than a Russian has medals.

The girl was still kicking the glass.

"Give her a light sedative."

The assistant threw a switch. A hissing sound was heard, and a mist swirled through the chamber.

"And give her something to wear . . ."

Another switch—and a pile of bright clothing fell into the chamber from above.

The girl snatched the clothes up and looked at them, frowning.

"Teno akta chtaman aasi n ometka!" she said as she began to put the clothes on, unhurriedly and without embarrassment.

Munro moved closer. Somethow the sight of the

beautiful girl slipping into a knit-and-plastic skintight tunic was even more exciting than seeing her nude, or almost nude.

"This thing solid?" he asked Mactilburgh.

"Unbreakable," said the scientist.

Munro smiled at the girl, who frowned back at him while she struggled with her clothes.

"If you want to get out, you're going to have to develop those communication skills," Munro taunted.

He was answered by a fist—the girl's, rammed straight through the glass.

She leaned out of the chamber, still only half dressed, and grabbed Munro by the front of his military tunic, picking him up so that his medals rattled.

*AaaoooGGGGaaa!* An alarm went off.

The girl banged Munro against the side of the chamber and then dropped him onto the floor.

She reached around the side of the chamber and unlocked it, then stepped out, still slightly wobbly on her long and shapely legs.

*AaaoooGGGGaaa!*

Two burly security guards burst into the lab.

The girl sent them flying, each toward an opposite wall.

Mactilburgh and his assistant backed into the corner. Mactilburgh's face showed terror mixed with admiration. His assistant's, terror only.

A phalanx of ten security guards with plastic shields and stun guns rushed into the lab.

## The Fifth Element

They surrounded the girl. She studied them for a moment, then backed up.

One step, two.

The guards moved forward. The girl was trapped in the far corner of the lab.

Then she turned and jumped *through* the wall, as if it were made of paper.

"Perfect!" breathed Mactilburgh, undismayed by the near total destruction of his laboratory.

It was public money, after all.

# 9

"AFTER HER!" CRIED THE CHIEF OF SECURITY. IT WAS HIS JOB AT stake, after all.

He sent his men in teams of two through the hole in the wall, directing them up to search every corner of the floor.

It was only a matter of time, he knew. The girl—or whatever she was—was trapped. He had shut down the elevators and the Central Lab was on the 450th floor.

"Do we have Deadly Force Authorization?" one of the security guards asked as he sprinted down a corridor.

His partner laughed. It was a joke. DFA was standard operating procedure for any unauthorized activity in the Central Laboratories. Or anywhere in Manhattan, for that matter.

Which was why, when the girl burst into view at

---

61

the end of the corridor, neither guard hesitated before opening fire.

*Bratabratabratabrat!*

*Bratabratabratabrat!*

Dodging the bullets, the girl looked up. A grille covered a ventilation duct in the ceiling.

*Bratabratabratabrat!*

She jumped up, grabbed the grille and flung it at the guards.

They ducked, firing wildly.

*Bratabratabratabrat!*

When they opened their eyes, she was gone.

"Got her!"

"No you didn't. I got her!"

"Neither of us did. She's gone!"

The guards peered up into the ventilation duct. They saw a scurry of movement at the far end of the shaft.

"After you," said one.

"No, after you," said the other.

Just then the Chief of Security arrived on the scene. Looking up, he saw immediately what was happening.

"You two! Come with me," he said, pulling himself up into the open shaft.

"After you."

"No, after you."

"Come on, dammit—move!"

As swiftly and surely as a cat, the red-haired girl (if indeed she was a girl) scurried through the vent shaft, looking for a way out.

Even though she moved at lightning speed, her face showed no sign of panic.

Her green eyes were clear. Her ruby lips were parted in a slight smile.

Behind her could be heard the clumsy scraping and kicking of the security guards, getting closer and closer.

The narrow shaft turned right, then left.

Turned up, then down.

With each turn the duct got smaller, until the girl was on all fours, and then crawling on her belly.

She was as fast on her belly as she had been on her feet!

Then she reached the end.

Punto. Finito. Period. A barred steel grille.

Through it she could see blue sky.

She smiled and kicked out the grille.

It spun off into empty space.

She slipped through the hole, and stepped out onto a narrow ledge.

The ledge was eleven inches wide. It went around the 454th floor of the Central Technologies Building, which took up an entire block on 55th Street in Manhattan.

The girl looked down.

Below, she could see hovering swarms of air cars and taxis, scooting between the towers.

And far below them, the detritus and litter that was the "midden" of modern post-industrial society, the uncollected trash of five hundred years that was easier to build on than to move or collect.

There was a rattle and scraping in the duct; footsteps and out-of-breath voices.

The girl moved a few steps farther out on the ledge.

She walked easily, as if she had no fear of heights. Her green eyes flashed as she took in the spectacular view of mid-millennial Manhattan.

The subways now ran vertically as well as horizontally, trains of cars supplementing and connecting the antiquated elevators.

The office buildings were interspersed with the skeletons of the "racktowers," where space was rented for the modular apartments that could be unplugged and moved at the owner's wish. The higher you lived, the more you paid.

The street was just a smudge, far, far below. No one lived there except the homeless and the outlaws who crept through the garbage, feeding on the trash and debris that fell from above.

The trickle-down theory at work.

If the scene was new to the girl, she didn't show it. She hardly seemed to notice. She reached into one of the pockets on her skimpy outfit and pulled out the broken handle. She looked at it and shook her head, then put it back.

*Bratabratabratabrat!*

Shots ricocheted off the wall and the ledge, and the girl crept around the corner of the building, out of the line of fire.

———

A head stuck out of the shaft.

It was the Chief of Security. He looked out, then down—then turned pale and pulled his head back in.

He turned to the two men right behind him.

"Follow her!"

A security guard stuck his head out. A hand and foot followed. He took one step out onto the narrow ledge, then turned and clambered back into the ventilation shaft.

"No way," he said flatly.

The second guard took one look and pulled back.

"No way."

The Chief of Security had been preparing a series of threats in his mind. He reconsidered and filed them away.

He popped open his cell phone. "We need a flying unit here!" he said.


*WOOWEEEWOOOWEEE!*

Siren wailing, lights flashing, a police cruiser zoomed up between the buildings. Swarms of cabs moved out of the way.

The chief leaned out far enough to point, and the police cruiser shut off its siren. Hovering silently, it crept slowly toward the corner of the building.

"This.is.the.police," said a robotic amplified voice.

"We.are.processing.your.identification."

Actually it wasn't a robot, but one of the two officers in the car, who had learned to imitate a robot through a post-academy mail order course.

He could see the perp standing on the narrow ledge. A pretty girl, in a very bright and very scanty outfit.

"She has no file!" said his partner, tapping the glass on the cruiser's computer terminal.

"Please.put.up.your.arms.and.follow.our. instructions," said the driver in his best robotic voice.

The girl seemed only too happy to comply.

She smiled and raised her arms. She stood on her tiptoes, looked down 450 stories, and—

"Christ!" said both cops at once. "She dove off!"

# 10

"LET ME OFF OVER THERE, PLEASE! THAT ENTRANCE ON THE LEFT, at the corner."

Korben yanked at the wheel of the cab, turning so fast that his gyros moaned, and cut under two lanes of traffic, expertly avoiding a fender-bender, a side swipe and a rear-ender, while ignoring the curses of a fellow cabbie.

He bobbled to a hovering stop at an entrance ledge high above the 44th Street Corridor, where what had once been 44th Street lay beneath twenty feet of midden trash.

"Wow," said the fare, a turquoise-suited businessman. "Where'd you learn to drive like that?"

"The last war," Korben said drily. "And the one before that."

"Awesome." The fare swiped his card through the slot, and the decal speakers in Korben's cab all started up at once, a chorus of tiny robot voices:

*"Please.make.sure.your.belongings.are . . ."*

*"While.in.New.York.visit.the . . ."*
*"Direct.any.complaints.or . . ."*

The fare opened the door.

"Hey," said Korben. "Aren't you forgetting something?"

The fare checked the seat behind him. "What?"

"The tip."

"I don't tip," said the fare, stepping out onto the entrance ledge. "It's against my principles."

"Great," said Korben, roaring off. "How often do you get to meet a true man of principle!"


Leaving the 44th, Korben cruised north, looking for a new fare. Cabs were hailed by balloons released by doormen, or by flashing lights at the entrance locks of the big corporations.

He was cruising at a little over 400 floors, watching the ledges out of the corners of his eyes, when—

CRASH!

Something hit the roof of the cab.

The impact tripped all the sensors, and the cab automatically droned: "You.have.just.had.an.accident."

"No shit!" Korben muttered, struggling to regain control of his careening cab. He glanced over his shoulder and saw to his amazement that someone had fallen into the cab, through the roof!

He stabilized his gyros and pulled over to the

side, out of the traffic. He hovered in the shadow of a parapet as the cab's voice droned on: "Four.points.have.been.temporarily removed . . . You.have.one.point.left.on.your.license."

*Great!* He sighed and looked into the back seat to assess the damage. Korben figured he had been hit by a "faller," one of midtown Manhattan's hundred or so suicides every day.

But if this was a suicide, it was an unsuccessful one.

The whatever-or-whoever-it-was had smashed through the crummy Plexiflex roof of the cab, and was lying on the back seat in a heap of legs and arms. Awfully pretty legs and arms, as a matter of fact!

"Any survivors?" Korben asked—and caught his breath.

A girl sat up in the pile of debris on the back seat of his cab. She was, for lack of a better word, beautiful. More than beautiful, in fact.

Heavenly.

There was a little blood on her face from a cut lip, but other than that she seemed miraculously unharmed.

Korben leaned over and wiped the blood off her mouth with his sleeve.

Her eyes were so green . . .

Korben's heart stopped and he felt like the cab was spinning.

Her hair was bright red . . .

She smiled.

---

He felt he ought to say *something*. But what does one say to a spectacularly pretty girl who just fell out of the sky?

"Hi," he said. "Nice hair."

"Akina delutan," the girl replied, with a broad smile, as if Korben had just said the cleverest thing she had ever heard. "Nou shan. Djela—Boom!"

"Boom?" queried Korben.

"Bada boom!" the girl said, clapping her hands.

Korben looked up through the demolished roof of his cab. He could see a blue police cruiser approaching, its lights flashing.

"Yeah," he said. "Big Bada Boom."

"YOU.HAVE.AN.UNAUTHORIZED.PAS-SENGER," growled the police cruiser in a demented robotic screech as it hovered in front of Korben's cab. "WE.ARE.GOING.TO.ARREST. HER.PLEASE.LEAVE.YOUR.HANDS.ON.THE. WHEEL.THANK.YOU.FOR.YOUR.COOPERA-TION."

Korben had had enough experience with New York's "finest" to know their reputation for trigger-happy un-professionalism.

He left his hands on the wheel in plain sight.

"Sorry, hon," he said over his shoulder. "But I think this is your ride. We'd better do what they say."

The police cruiser moved in clumsily, mag-locking onto the cab.

Huge guns pointed through every window of

the police cruiser, and behind every gun barrel were two black, beady eyes.

Cops.

The cruiser's doors slid open, and a hydraulic Felon-net emerged, complete with a set of automatic handcuffs, opened and beckoning.

Korben felt lousy.

He felt twice as lousy when he looked into the back seat and saw the tears in the girl's eyes.

Big beautiful green eyes.

"Sorry," he said.

Instead of answering, she pointed at one of the many stickers plastered on the doors and windows of Korben's cab.

It was a dial 1–800-ORPHAN sticker. It showed a kid's pleading eyes and below them, two words:

PLEASE HELP.

Was she trying to communicate?

"Don't!" Korben said. "Don't put me in this position. I can't!"

The girl nodded and pointed again to the sticker.

PLEASE HELP.

"I got only one point left on my license, and I need it to get to the garage," Korben pleaded. "It's my six-month overhaul. Understand?"

The girl seemed to understand the extraordinary power she had over Korben's emotions. She smiled wistfully, wiped a tear from an eye, and pointed to the sticker again.

PLEASE HELP.

---

71

"Finger's going to kill me," Korben muttered.

He shut off the meter on the cab.

"THANK.YOU.FOR.YOUR.COOPERA-TION," the police said, as Korben hit the null switch under his dash, momentarily overriding the maglock.

"You're welcome," said Korben—

And he floored the gyros, spinning the cab free, and sending the police cruiser into an asymmetric tailspin, knocking it against the side of the building two stories below.

"WE'VE.BEEN.HIT!" squawked the cruiser, its automatics kicking in. "REQUEST.BACK.UP! IN.PURSUIT!"

"One.point.has.been.removed.from.your.license," said the cab in Korben's ear.

"I wondered when you were going to chime in," muttered Korben.

He spun the wheel, rocketing around a corner and down six stories, away from the flashing lights of the cruiser.

A flurry of curses, honks and shouts followed him.

"You.have.no.points.left," the cab continued. "You.are.unauthorized.to.operate.this.vehicle. Would.you.please . . ."

The voice died suddenly as Korben ripped the speaker from the ceiling and tossed it out the window, into the open back of a passing pickup.

"I hate it when people cry," he said. In the rearview mirror, he saw the red-haired girl, watching the commotion with a slightly bemused smile.

She was so beautiful that he could barely tear his eyes away, back to the darting aerial traffic.

"I got no defense, you know!"

# 11

A FEW BLOCKS AWAY, UNIT 47 OF THE 2345 PRECINCT WAS IN line for the McDonald's take-out window when the radio crackled into life.

"All units in Sector 12 full alert converge on vector 21."

"Vector, sector," said the young cop riding shotgun. "I never can get it straight."

His older partner at the wheel spoke into the mike. "Unit 47, we're on our way . . ."

He hung up the mike, and finished, ". . . as soon as we eat some lunch. Get the burgers, kid."

The younger cop spoke into another mike, this one hovering patiently in the air outside the cruiser, waiting for an order. "One Big Mac with regular fries, with Diet Coke. One Quarter Pounder with large fries and a caffeine-free Diet Cherry Coke. Copy?"

"That's One Big Mac with regular fries, with Diet Coke. One Quarter Pounder with large fries and a caffeine-free Diet Cherry Coke."

"Roger. Over and out."

The line of hovering aerial vehicles inched forward. The young cop turned to his partner. "Shouldn't we be responding to that call?"

The older cop shook his head. "I'm too tired, too old and too hungry to go chasing some hotrod call."

The cruiser pulled up to the take-out window.

"And I'm definitely too thirsty," said the older cop, reaching across for his tray of cokes.

A tray of burgers followed. He was reaching for it, when—

WHAM!

—it disappeared as a speeding yellow cab slipped between the window and the cruiser, taking off the side of both.

The cops looked at one another, and then at the battered yellow cab disappearing between the skyscrapers.

"Why don't you sit up here?" said Korben, patting the seat beside him. "Long as we're illegal anyway."

The girl climbed into the front seat. Her colorful outfit was intriguingly revealing.

She combed her red hair with her fingers.

*WOOWEEEWOOOWEEE!*

Behind the speeding cab, the sirens were getting louder. Korben slashed across and over six lanes of traffic, then doubled back two blocks, spun up six stories, then slowed to an idling pace.

"If they don't chase you after a mile," he said, "they don't chase you. Believe me."

He turned a corner, and suddenly six sky blue police cruisers burst out of an alleyway in hot pursuit.

"Maybe it's two miles," he muttered, flooring the turbines and twisting the gyros to full evasion mode.

"Klaatu barata nikto," said the girl.

"Lady, I'm sorry," said Korben. "I only speak two languages: English, and bad English."

The six police cruisers separated into two groups of three, one to the left and one to the right.

Korben threw the cab into a spin, straight down through the canyons toward a roof garden far below.

The cruisers followed.

Korben pulled up at the last moment.

Four of the cruisers pulled up—

WHUMP! WHUMP! Two of the cruisers spun out and buried themselves in the soft synthetic rooftop dirt.

Korben headed straight downtown, with four police cruisers hot on his tail.

"Maica lota muni," said the girl.

"Listen, lady," he said. "I'm all for conversation, but can you shut up a minute? This is a little tricky . . ."

The four cruisers were closing in, their high-powered police turbos whining.

The cab's screen was beeping.

Korben turned it on.

ATTACK MODE! ATTACK MODE! ATTACK MODE!

Korben turned to his passenger. "I don't know what you did to piss them off . . ."

ENGAGED! ENGAGED! ENGAGED!

"But they are really pissed off. Hold on."

Korben doubled the gyros while cutting in the braking blasters: an old air combat trick.

The cab groaned in protest but made the turn.

"I think we're safe for a while," Korben said. Then he looked in the rearview mirror.

Two police cruisers were still closing in.

"I tried to play it soft, boys," Korben whispered. "Too bad you don't appreciate it."

He cut his hoverjets and pushed the stick forward.

"We'll be safe in the smog. If we reach it."

Korben's cruiser turned turtle and dove—straight down, through the startled scurrying cabs and flivvers and maglev limos.

He powered up at the last minute, just above the garbage that covered the street.

A right, a left, through the noxious methane mist.

Then a dead end.

"Daya deo bono dato!" said the girl. She seemed pleased with the excitement. "Dalutan!"

"If there's one thing I don't need," said Korben, "It's advice on how to drive."

Turning a sudden loop, Korben whipped the

cab sideways. Then he pressed the stick to one side with his knee and turned off his maglev arrester—another old fighter pilot trick—so that the cab turned sideways.

Steering with uncanny precision, Korben threaded the cab through an alley so tight that the ancient bricks scraped the light off the top.

The first police cruiser was a foot wider. It sped in and then scraped to a screeching halt.

The second cruiser braked just in time.

"Shit! Attention all patrol cars!"

Then backed up and made a U-turn.

The deepening haze and smog that clung to the ground level of the city mercifully obscured the generations of litter and debris—the urban *midden* that covered the streets to a depth of between twenty and forty feet.

No one lived down here.

That was what the young cop thought.

Then he saw the figures, almost human, clothed in rags and skins, climbing up and around, slipping and sliding over and between the enormous piles of rotting garbage.

He shuddered.

"Look at this!" he said to his partner. "The garbage collectors go out, or what?"

"Yeah," said the older cop, sarcastically. "They been out a week already."

It was of course a joke. The garbage collectors

had been out for a generation, ever since the city had discovered it was cheaper to let the trash build up than haul it to a landfill.

Since the city soared upward faster than the trash, it created no problem for those living in the upper levers.

And the trash was handy as a dwelling and scavenging place for the drop-outs—literally—those who couldn't afford to soar upward with the city.

It was retropostneodarwinism in action, and though it made perfect economic sense, the young cop found it, well—

Disgusting.

The piles seemed to sigh, emitting clouds of steaming stink. But where was the fugitive cabbie?

He was supposed to be trapped in this dead-end alcove. But there was nothing here but a vertical billboard, advertising a long-forgotten company called "IBM."

The young cop scanned the billboard, which was fifty feet high but only ten wide, not nearly wide enough to hide a cab.

"Where'd he go?" he asked his partner.

The older cop motioned down, toward the midden.

"Down, I guess," he said. "Must have lost his gyros. Not our job to sift through that crap for bodies. Let's go get another burger."

Korben was looking up, even as the cops were looking down.

His cab was behind the sign, hovering on its tail—another old fighter pilot trick. It was expensive in electrics, but effective.

Uncomfortable, too. The girl and Korben were jammed together in the front seat.

Well, not exactly uncomfortable. The girl had a nice warm smell that overcame the garbage.

"We'll wait here till things calm down a bit," Korben whispered. "You mind?"

The girl grabbed his shirt collar and whispered in his ear. "Priest . . ."

Korben studied her. She seemed weak. Her green eyes were almost closed.

"Priest . . ." she said again.

"You're not that bad!" Korben said. "Come on, we'll get you to a doctor."

"Vee-toe," said the girl. "Cor-knee-lee-us."

It sounded almost like a name. "Vito Cornelius?"

The girl nodded.

Then fainted.

# 12

"YES?"

The door was opened by an old man, small, with a face as round as a one-franc piece, and a shock of white hair.

His visitor was a strong, scarred man short on hair but long on nervousness.

In his arms was a girl. She appeared to be sleeping.

"Excuse me," Korben said, "I'm looking for a priest."

"Weddings are one floor down, my son," said the priest. "And congratulations."

He closed the door.

It opened again—kicked in.

"She's not my bride," said Korben. "She's my fare. She's looking for a Vito Cornelius. According to the phone guide he lives here."

"That's me," said the priest, buckling his robe more tightly around him as he stared at the two intruders. "But I don't know who she is."

The girl was wearing a bright, revealing jumpsuit and her shoulder-length hair was fiery red.

The priest regarded her suspiciously. "Where did you find her?"

"She . . . dropped in on me," Korben said.

He held the girl out toward the priest and her arm dropped to one side. There was a tattoo on her wrist.

Four elements connected by lines.

When the priest saw it, the color drained from his face.

He looked down at the scarred and scratched symbol of the four elements on his antique brass belt buckle. It matched her tattoo exactly.

"The Fifth Element!" he breathed, and sank to the floor, unconscious.

Korben stepped all the way into the apartment, letting the door slide shut behind him.

"Finger's going to kill me!" he muttered, looking for a place to set down the girl.


SLAP. Cornelius awoke.

He was staring into a battered but kindly, tough but intelligent mug.

"Who are you?"

"I brought the girl, remember?"

Cornelius sat up. "Girl?"

Then he remembered. The Fifth Element.

"Yeah!" Korben was saying. "She dropped in

on me. I mean, on my taxi. Talking this bizarre language."

Cornelius shook his head, so slowly that it seemed almost a new style of prayer.

"Not bizarre. The divine language. The most ancient language. Spoken through the Universe before time was Time. The Fifth Element, the Supreme . . ."

Cornelius looked at the girl who lay stretched out on the couch, her red hair gleaming, and suddenly it dawned on him:

"He's—a *she*!"

"You noticed," said Korben.

His sarcasm was lost on the priest, who was all but kneeling before the sleeping girl. "It's a miracle! There's not a moment to lose! Wake her up, but be gentle about it! This woman is mankind's most precious possession!"

"She is?"

"She is—perfect!"

And Cornelius ran out of the room.

Korben knelt by the girl's side.

He raised an arm to slap her awake, then changed his mind.

He lowered the hand slowly. With his fingertips, he touched her cheek.

Her skin was as soft and fragile as the petal of a rose. It was hard to believe she had fallen through the roof of his cab, almost unharmed.

"Perfect," Korben whispered.

"It's a miracle!"

The novice, David, looked up from the cassock he was mending with his favorite ancient device, a needle and thread.

Father Cornelius had just burst into the room, out of breath and red-faced.

"Miracle?" David asked. "Where?"

Father Cornelius opened the closet door

"I can't wear these clothes," he said. "This calls for dignity!"

The closet was hung with cassocks. They were all identical to the one David was mending; identical, in fact, to the one Father Cornelius was wearing.

"I have to dress the part!" cried Cornelius, disappearing into the closet as David looked on, shaking his head in wonder.


The girl wouldn't wake up.

Korben touched her cheek, then her other cheek.

Suddenly, on an impulse that surprised even him, he bent down and kissed her gently on the lips.

That worked.

Her eyes snapped open.

Korben felt something cold, and sat up suddenly.

It was his own gun jammed under his chin.

The girl had pulled it from his shoulder holster in a single swift movement.

"Eto akta gamat!"

"I'm sorry," said Korben. "It's just that . . ."

*Just that what?* her eyes seemed to ask.

Embarrassed, Korben stumbled on. He wasn't particularly good with girls (although they usually didn't seem to notice). "I was told to wake you up gently, so I figured . . ."

The girl looked puzzled. She lowered the gun.

"You're right," said Korben. "I'm wrong. I shouldn't have kissed you. Especially since we haven't been formally introduced, and . . ."

He fumbled in the pockets of his vest and pulled out a cheap, blinking plastic business card.

"Here. It's a bit late, but my name is Korben. Korben Dallas. I'm a cab driver. Call me any time. You don't need to jump off a building to catch a cab, you know. Just call . . ."

The girl hesitated for a moment, then snatched the card out of his hand.

With an unexpected smile.

"Father!"

"Mumphh."

David could tell where Father Cornelius was by watching the rippling of the cassocks in the closet. It was like tracking a whale underwater.

A very small, very determined whale.

"Father, will you please explain what is going on?"

"The Supreme Being," said Father Cornelius,

his voice muffled by the yards of dusty cloth that hung in the closet.

"The what?"

"The Fifth Element! Here in our parish!"

Cornelius emerged with a clean cassock, holding it in front of him like a schoolgirl checking out her prom dress.

"It's a miracle!" he said.


"And what's your name?" Korben asked the girl.

She was studying the card he had given her.

Korben pointed to his name on the card. "Name!"

She brightened, seeming to understand.

"Leeloo Minai Lekarariba-Laminai-Tchaii Ekbat De Sebat," she said matter-of-factly.

"Hey," said Korben, struggling to take it all in. "That's . . . cute. Do you have a nickname? Something a little . . . shorter?"

"Leeloo."

Korben stared into her deep green eyes. They were like a sea in which he was eager to drown. Her flame-red hair was like a fire in which he desperately wanted to be consumed.

He was falling in love.

"Leeloo," he repeated. "That's really . . . cute."


Father Cornelius and David burst into the living room—and found themselves staring into the barrel of Korben's gun, held on them by the girl.

"Appipulai Leeloo Minai," Cornelius said.

The girl lowered the gun. "Cor knee lee us?"

He bowed. "At your service."

She started to laugh. It was a childish, infectious laugh that brought a smile to the old priest's face, and to Korben's as well.

Only the young novice, David, was frowning. He had never been so close to such a desirable creature. It bothered him that she was so . . . sexy.

He turned to the priest. "Are you sure she's the Supreme Being?"

"Absolutely," said Cornelius. "There are the Four Elements on her wrist!"

David bowed low, while Leeloo extended her thin wrist for his examination.

Meanwhile, Cornelius took Korben's thick wrist in his two small hands and steered him toward the door.

"Thanks so much for your help, Mr. . . ?"

"Dallas," said Korben. "Korben Dallas. But—"

Korben looked back over his shoulder. Leeloo was no longer laughing. She was watching him with sad eyes.

"Yes," babbled the priest, "that's fine. Thank you very much, a thousand times over!"

"Think I might call to check up on her?" Korben asked as the apartment door slid open. "You know, to see if she's better?"

"She's fine, really," said Father Cornelius as he expertly hustled Korben through the door. "Don't

worry. She just needs some rest. She's had a very
long trip!"

"I know," Korben said. "I was there when she
arrived."

He was neatly deposited in the hallway.

The door was just about to slide shut when he
checked it with his hand, tripping the safety override.

"Excuse me. One other thing, Father. She said
something to me a while ago and I didn't really get
it. Akta gamat?"

"Akta gamat," repeated Cornelius, hitting the
safety override. "It means 'Never without my permission.'"

"That's what I thought," said Korben as the
door slid shut in his face.


"Evening!" said Korben to the robot doorman.

It was a half hour later. He had taken the cab
back to the garage, and he was returning to his
lonely apartment halfway up the towers of the city.
Not high enough for the truly clean air, but above
the worst of the smell.

"Evening," he said to his neighbor in the hallway.

"Fuck you," said the nasty neighbor. It was
what he always said to everybody.

"Thanks," said Korben wearily. "You too."

He slipped into his tiny apartment module.

"Meeeow!"

The cat came running and started rubbing against his leg.

"Oh, God, I forgot your food! I'm really sorry!" Korben turned and pressed a button on the wall. It was directly connected to a fast-food restaurant. "How about a nice Thai nosh to apologize? How does that sound?"

"Meow."

The phone rang. "Hello?"

"Hey, bud," growled Finger's voice. "I'm waiting all day here at the garage."

"Finger, man," muttered Korben. "I'm sorry. Listen, the cab is fine. Purring like a cat."

"Yeah? Well, if that's the case why don't you let me hear it?"

"Okay. Look," said Korben, "I was on my way over, but I had a fare fall into my lap. You know, one of those big fares you just can't resist?"

Finger was still suspicious. "How big?"

"About five-foot-nine," said Korben, pulling a cigarette from his vest. "Green eyes, long legs, great skin. You know? Perfect."

He tried to light a match.

It sputtered damply and went out.

"Uh huh," said Finger. "I see! And this perfect fare—she's got, like, a name?"

"Yeeaaahhh," said Korben dreamily. "Leeloo."

# 13

"WHAT'S SHE DOING!?" DAVID DEMANDED.

He couldn't take his eyes off her.

First she had walked nearly nude out of the shower.

Now she was sitting at the computer, wearing only a skimpy towel, wolfing down fried chicken.

Leeloo was surfing around the Internet so fast that the modem cable was smoking, the hard drive was whining, the chip was barking like a dog.

On the screen, data was scrolling past in a steady stream.

"She's learning our history!" said Cornelius. "The last five thousand years that she missed. She's been out of circulation a while, you know!"

Both men looked over, startled, as Leeloo broke into laughter. Her laugh was a bright, musical sound, like the laughter of children, totally without malice or cruelty.

"What are you *laughing* about?" Cornelius asked. What could she find in the bloody history of humanity's last five thousand years that could be the slightest bit amusing?

"Nap Oh Leon," said Leeloo.

"What the heck is funny about Napoleon?" David asked.

"Small!" chirped Leeloo. "So small!"

Still giggling, she tossed two more KwikChick capsules into the microwave.

The microwave scanned the capsules, clicked on the timer, and turned itself on.

"Uh, Father," said David. "I know she's been through a lot. But we don't have much time. The Ultimate Evil is getting closer and closer."

"Yes, of course," said Cornelius.

*Ding!*

Leeloo opened the microwave. The capsule had expanded into a steaming plate heaped with chicken and vegetables.

She set the chicken dinner beside the computer and sat down in front of it, scrolling with one hand and eating with the other. Her appetite seemed bottomless.

"Leeloo," Cornelius began. "I'm sorry to interrupt you, but . . ."

He held up the broken handle she had given him.

"The case?"

Leeloo shrugged, starting on her second chicken dinner. The screen scrolled faster.

"The case with the Sacred Stones," Father Cornelius went on. "You were supposed to have it."

"San Agmat chay bet," said Leeloo. "Envolet!"

"The case was stolen?"

Leeloo nodded, seemingly unperturbed. She helped herself to more chicken.

"Who in God's name would do such a thing?" Cornelius asked, shocked.


Zorg, that's who.

At that very moment, the galaxy's cruelest financier was lurching crabwise across his warehouse in his best Byronic limp, musing on how to use his zillions most strategically, to the detriment of all that is wholesome and good.

For Zorg the equation was simple: whatever course of action gave the most benefit to himself and the least to humankind, was always to be preferred.

He was lost in these lofty thoughts when his most valued assistant scurried closer.

"Excuse me, sir," said Zorg's right arm, Right Arm. "The council is worried about the economy heating up. They wondered if it would be possible to fire five hundred thousand. I thought maybe from one of the smaller companies, where no one would notice. Like one of the cab companies."

Zorg thought for a moment. "Fire a million."

"But sir, five hundred thousand is all they need."

Zorg turned slowly and eyed his assistant.

The thin scar that ran across his face was reddening. His right eyelid was beginning to flutter, a sign that he was about to fly into a vicious rage.

The message clearly written on Zorg's face was not lost on Right Arm. "A million! Fine, sir! Sorry to have disturbed you, sir!"


Meanwhile, back on the 323rd level of a middle-income racktower, in a spartan monastic apartment cubicle, Father Cornelius was talking to himself:

"Who would do such a thing? Hmmmmm . . ."

His young novice, David, entered the room with a bundle of clothing. Women's clothing.

"There was this guy with a limp . . . and a scar," Cornelius mused aloud. "Came by a month ago. Said he was an art dealer. . . . Asked all these questions about the Sacred Stones."

David handed the clothing to Leeloo, who was seated at the computer, still clad most fetchingly in only a towel.

"I didn't know your size," he apologized. "And I found this makeup box."

"I didn't think anything about it at the time," continued Cornelius absentmindedly. "What was his name? I'm so bad with names. . . ."

Leeloo stood up, smiling. She stripped off the towel and threw it into the corner.

Father Cornelius and David stared, transfixed.

She was nude.

Wonderfully, beautifully, perfectly nude.

"They really made her, uh . . ." David stammered.

"Perfect," finished Cornelius. "Yes, I know."

The two men turned away as Leeloo slipped into the clothing David had brought.

She twirled and admired herself in front of an imaginary mirror (since Father Cornelius kept no mirror in his apartment). It was almost as if she could see herself from without—

"Domo danko," she said to David, squeezing his hand.

David turned around and grinned stupidly. The clothes fit perfectly.

"Leeloo?" said Father Cornelius. "The Stones! Time is running out. We must get them back."

She nodded and sat back down at the computer.

"Ikset-kiba. Me imanetaba oum dalat!"

Father Cornelius didn't know whether to be astonished or overjoyed by her words—or both.

"You do?" he said. "You know exactly where the Sacred Stones are!?"

So did someone—or something—else.

At least, they thought they did.

A group of handsome, godlike warriors entered Zorg's warehouse, buzzed in by the security 'bot, and crowded onto the elevator.

The handsomest of the handsome warriors, Aknot, carried a metal case in his hand.

It was missing a handle.

The elevator door opened. With his warriors close behind, Aknot started down the long echoing corridor.

Zorg and Right Arm waited at the end.

"Aknot, is that you?" asked Zorg when he saw the approaching warriors.

Aknot nodded. His handsome face was illuminated by a perfect, godlike smile.

"What an ugly mug!" said Zorg. "It doesn't suit you at all. Take it off!"

Aknot shrugged. His face melted away, revealing the twisted, froglike, monstrous, misshapen, crapulous, crepuscular, uncouth, carpified, face of—

—a Mangalore. The ugliest race in the Galaxy.

"That's better!" said Zorg. "Never be ashamed of who—and what—you are!"

Aknot nodded. He gave a signal to his warriors and they, too, relaxed and let their faces melt away, revealing the Mangalore hideousness underneath.

Right Arm tried to hide his disgust.

"So what if the Federal Army crushed your entire race!" said Zorg. "So what if the government scattered your people to the wind. What doesn't kill you makes you stronger, eh?"

He opened the crate by his side. It was filled with laser rifles.

"Your time for revenge is at hand. Voila—"

Zorg held up one of the rifles.

"The ZF1!"

Zorg hefted the weapon in his small, grasping hands.

---

"It's light. The handle's adjustable for easy carrying; good for righties and lefties . . ."

Zorg threw a switch on the side of the stock. The weapon glowed and hummed with what seemed an intelligent, if malicious, anticipation of havoc and destruction.

"Ideal for quick, discreet interventions," Zorg went on, winding into the smooth sales pitch that distinguished one of the galaxy's leading arms dealers.

He nodded at two warehousemen, who hurried to set up a mannequin at the far end of the corridor.

"The last word in firepower!" barked Zorg. "Titanium recharger, 3000 round clip. With the replay button—another Zorg innovation—it's even easier. One shot . . ."

Taking quick aim, Zorg fired at the faraway mannequin.

*BRAP*! THUNK!

A hit.

"Then hit Replay and send every following shot to the same location!"

Zorg spun around on his heel, firing the ZF1 wildly into the air as he made a complete circle.

*BRAP A RAP AA RAP AA RAP AA RAP AA RAP AA RAP*!

The Mangalores all hit the deck. So did Right Arm.

THUNK A THUNK A THUNK A THUNK A THUNK A THUNK!

---

Every single shot hit the mannequin, rocking it on its stand.

The Mangalores, including Aknot, got back to their feet.

So did Right Arm.

"And to finish the job," continued Zorg, "all the usual Zorg oldies but goodies—"

A small missile streaked across the room and buried itself in the mannequin. "The rocket launcher."

A tongue of flame licked the floor. "The always efficient flame thrower; my favorite . . ."

A grenade arced into the air, exploding into a net which fell over the smoldering mannequin. "Our famous net launcher!"

A flurry of arrows flew out, some sticking into the mannequin and some exploding on impact. "The arrow launcher, with exploding or poisonous gas heads—very practical!

"And for the grand finale—"

A thin stream of gas hissed out of the rifle, chilling the air as it passed. "The all-new ice cube system!"

The mannequin, already blasted, riddled, punctured, charred, and stuck with arrows, froze and cracked into shards of dirty ice that fell into a mass on the warehouse floor.

Zorg tossed the weapon into Aknot's stubby hands.

He pointed to the four crates at the side of the corridor.

"Four full crates of ZF1s, delivered right on

time. What about you, my dear Aknot? Did you bring me what I asked you for?"

Aknot set the metal case on one of the crates.

Zorg touched it reverently.

"Magnificent!"

Aknot smiled.

As Zorg carefully, reverently, opened the case, his scarred face creased into a cruelly blissful smile—

Which faded suddenly as the case sprang open.

It was empty.


"What do you mean empty?" Cornelius asked.

Leeloo was laughing—that childish musical sound that was like the wind laughing through fields of flowers.

She explained in her musical language, while Cornelius translated for the young novice, David.

"She says that the Guardians were afraid of being attacked. The Sacred Stones were taken out of the case and given to someone they could trust, who took another route."

"Caupo ruta welso brak!" said Leeloo, and she bent down over the keyboard. The computer's search engines groaned.

"Leeloo's supposed to contact this person in a hotel," said Cornelius. "She's searching for the address."

But instead of a list of four-star hotels, the screen showed a map of . . . stars.

"Dot!" said Leeloo.

David bent down to look.

He followed her finger, then picked up the mouse and clicked twice where it pointed.

"Planet Fhloston, in the Angel constellation," he read.

Father Cornelius leaned back in his chair and breathed a sigh of relief.

"We're saved!"


"I'm screwed," said Zorg.

He closed the case.

"Empty is the *opposite* of full. This case is supposed to be full. Anyone care to explain?"

He fixed a blood-chilling stare on Aknot, who, since he was already cold blooded, was unimpressed.

"You asked for a case. We brought you a case."

Zorg's scar reddened. His eyelid twitched.

He lost it.

"A case with four stones in it! Not one! Not two or three, but four! Four stones! What the hell am I supposed to do with an empty case?"

Aknot's warriors backed up, lashed by the fury of Zorg's tirade. They clustered around their leader, their fingers on the triggers of their weapons, which, though not ZF1s, were still formidable.

Zorg and his assistants were unarmed.

Right Arm was beginning to look nervous.

"We are warriors, not merchants," said Aknot coldly.

"But you can still count," said Zorg. His voice had dropped back down to a faux-peaceful tone that was anything but soothing. He held up four fingers.

"Look. My fingers. Four stones, four crates. Zero stones . . ."

His voice rose to a shrill scream.

"Zero crates!"

He turned to his warehousemen. "Put everything back. We're outta here!"

The warehousemen hesitated. The Mangalore warriors held their weapons leveled on Zorg.

Aknot shook his head. "We risked out lives. I believe a little compensation is in order."

Zorg smiled. "So you are a merchant after all." He turned to his men. "Leave them one crate. For the cause."

Without another word, he lifted the empty case and walked out.

Right Arm followed.

Still under the guns of the Mangalores, the warehousemen lifted the three crates of laser rifles and scurried toward the elevator.


"I don't like warriors," said Zorg as he walked out of the warehouse, onto the street.

He handed the empty case to his right arm, Right Arm, who put it under his right arm.

"They're too narrow-minded!"

Right Arm nodded. He knew better than to respond. This was not a conversation; it was a lecture.

"No subtlety! Worse—they fight for hopeless causes. For honor! Honor has killed millions of creatures but hasn't saved a single one."

Right Arm nodded.

Even as Zorg spoke, a few hundred yards behind him, the Mangalores were opening the crate of rifles.

"You know what I *do* like, though?" Zorg continued, as he and Right Arm got into a waiting limo.

Right Arm nodded. He knew that all he had to do was listen.

"I like a killer! A dyed-in-the-wool killer. Cold blooded. Clean. Methodical. Thorough."

Right Arm nodded.

In the warehouse, the warriors gazed at the gleaming weapons. One of the warriors picked up a laser rifle and handed it to Aknot.

"A real killer," Zorg went on, "when he picked up the ZF1, would have immediately asked about the little red button on the bottom of the gun."

He knocked on the partition. "Drive on."

At the end of the block, in the top of the warehouse, Aknot turned over the gun.

He noticed the little red button.
It was flashing insistently.
He pressed it with a stubby lizardlike finger.
BAAAARRRROOOOOM!

Zorg smiled as the warehouse went up in flames
two blocks behind him. Smoke billowed out
through the streets, and there was silence.

Then the distant wail of sirens.

"Bring me the old priest," said Zorg.

Right Arm nodded.

# 14

THAI FLY BY WAS NOTHING IF NOT FAST.

Ten minutes after Korben's call, the little hovering mini-restaurant was secured to the window of his apartment.

It looked like a cross between a Chinese junk, a Viking raider and a giant red-enameled pooper scooper. But the smells that wafted up from its tiny kitchen were delicious.

Korben, seated at his table, and his cat, seated *on* the table, were sharing a single disposable plate of rice noodles, spring rolls and assorted Thai appetizers.

"So you forgive me?" Korben asked.

"Meow," said the cat, scarfing down another expensive sliver of sesame oil roasted fish.

The Thai cook knocked on the windowsill.

"You got a message," he said, pointing to the glass message tube that served all the modular apartments in this mega-racktower.

"I know," said Korben. He ignored the blinking light.

"Not going to open?"

"Later," said Korben.

"But could be important . . ." said the hovering restaurateur.

Korben shrugged. "Sure. Like the last two messages I got. The first one was from my wife, telling me she was leaving. The second was from my lawyer, telling me he was leaving too. With my wife."

"Oh!" said the Thai cook, "that *is* bad luck. But mathematically, luck must change! Grandfather say: 'It never rain every day!' This is good news guarantee! I bet you lunch!"

"Okay," said Korben. "It's a bet."

He pulled the message out of the tube and handed it to the Thai cook.

The cook opened the paper and read it with a smile that quickly faded to a frown.

"I lose bet," he said. "You're fired!"

Korben smiled. "At least I won lunch."

"Good philosophy," said the flyby cook, sharpening his chopping knife on the side of his hovering mini-kitchen. "See good in bad! I prepare number one dessert, especially for you and pussy."

"Meow," said the cat.

Dessert was also being served at Father Cornelius's spartan apartment across town.

Leeloo was finishing off her angel food cake, daintily sucking her elegant little fingertips, one by one.

Meanwhile, the novice, David, was seated at the computer. The search engines clanked and groaned, and the screen was filled with darting digits of data.

"I got it!" David cried triumphantly. "Everything we need to know about Fhloston Paradise—and a detailed blueprint of the entire hovering hotel."

"Good work, my son," said Father Cornelius. "Now all we need is a way to get there."

David scrolled on down, through reservations.

"It's not going to be easy," he said. "There's a big charity ball on Fhloston tomorrow. The flights have been full for months. And with all the celebrities, the hotel will be guarded like a fortress."

"There must be a way . . ." Cornelius was saying, when the doorbell rang.

He got to his feet. "I'll get it."

It was Right Arm with an armed guard. An ugly, intimidating armed guard.

Not that Father Cornelius was intimidated. A man who has been preparing all his life to battle the Ultimate Evil is rarely shaken by the lesser varieties.

"Father Cornelius?" asked Right Arm.

"My son?"

It was the first time anyone had ever called Right Arm "son." Even his own mother had called him "Hey You."

It took him a moment to recover his composure.

"Mr. Zorg would like a word with you."

"Mr. Who?"

A few minutes and a few thousand vertical feet later, Father Cornelius was ushered into a corner office high above Manhattan.

"Zorg," said Zorg, rising cordially to greet his guest. "Jean Baptiste Emmanuel Zorg. Nice to see you again, Father."

He motioned to a leather chair.

"Again?" Cornelius studied the scarred and delicately hideous face. "I remember you now. The so-called art dealer."

"I'm glad you got your memory back," said Zorg. "Because you are going to need it. Where are the Sacred Stones?"

"Why on Earth do the stones interest you?" asked Cornelius.

"On Earth!?!" Zorg chuckled. "Personally, the stones are of no interest to me. I'd rather sell weapons. But I have a customer for them. So tell me . . ."

"Even if I knew where the Sacred Stones were," said Cornelius, "I would never tell somebody like you."

Zorg looked offended. Or perhaps flattered. Or perhaps a little of both.

"Why? What's wrong with me?"

"I'm a priest," said Cornelius. "I'm here to serve life. All you want to do is destroy it."

Zorg shook his head pityingly.

"Ah, Father," he said in the tone one might use to a dense child, "you are so wrong. Let me explain."

He picked up a pitcher of ice water off a side table.

He poured a glass half full.

"Life, which you so nobly serve, comes from destruction, disorder and chaos. Look at this glass."

With one finger he pushed the glass toward the side of the counter.

"Here it is, peaceful. Serene. Boring. But if it is destroyed . . ."

He pushed the glass off the edge.

It smashed on the floor.

Immediately, the floor was swarming with tiny nanobots, cleaning up the splinters of broken glass and mopping up the water.

"Look at all these little things. So busy now! Notice how each one is useful. What a lovely ballet ensues, so full of form and color. So full of . . . life!"

"Life?" Cornelius watched scornfully. "They are robots."

Zorg poured water into another glass.

He pulled the stem off a cherry and dropped the cherry into the glass.

It sank.

"Yes, they are robots, but who designs them?" he asked Cornelius. "Builds them? Engineers, technicians, mechanics. Hundreds of people who will be able to feed their children tonight, so that those children can grow up to be big and strong—have children of their own, and so on and so forth, adding to the great chain of life!"

Cornelius sat in silence.

"So you see, Father, by creating a little destruction, I am, in fact, encouraging life. You and I are in the same business."

"Hardly," said Cornelius. "Destroying a glass is one thing. Killing people with the weapons you produce is quite another."

Zorg's dry laugh was as harsh as wind in dead leaves.

"Let me reassure you, Father, I could never kill as many people in my entire life as religion has killed in the past two thousand years."

He raised the glass. The cherry bobbed at the bottom like a severed head.

"Cheers."

He tipped the glass back and took a deep drink. The water disappeared.

Then the cherry disappeared.

Zorg's eyes grew wide. He dropped the glass. He pointed at the glass and then at his throat.

"You're choking?" asked Cornelius. He watched as Zorg fell, writhing, onto his massive teakwood desk.

Zorg's arm flailed about, reaching for the desktop communications console. His hand stabbed blindly at the row of buttons.

The phone lines lit.

The fax machine booted up.

The lights went on.

A CD recorder rose from a well in the desk.

A TV monitor emerged from the wall.

"Where's the robot to pat your back?" Cornelius asked. His voice was as dry, his tone as sarcastic as Zorg's had ever been. "Where's the engineer, or the mechanic—or their children, maybe. All of whom you claim owe their very lives to you?"

Zorg's hand continued to stab blindly at the console.

The door to the office slid shut, cutting off the two men from all hope of outside assistance.

A panel opened in the ceiling and a cage descended.

In it was a fat multicolored alien beast, a slug-like reptile with a trunk like an elephant's: Zorg's pet—a Souliman Aktapan named Picasso.

The cage landed on the desk, and Picasso stuck his slimy trunk through the bars to lick (or whatever) the twitching hand of his half-dead master.

Cornelius got up from his leather chair and walked around the desk.

Slowly.

"We were not put upon this Earth to destroy each other, Mr. Zorg, but to reflect the goodness of life—the infinite possibilities of life."

He paused to admire the view out the window, turning his back on Zorg's all but lifeless form.

"That is our mission—and not to decide who lives and who dies. And if you forget that . . ."

Cornelius picked up the stem of the cherry from the desktop, where Zorg had dropped it.

". . . nature will remind you. See how all your so-called power counts for nothing? See how your entire empire of destruction comes crashing down because of a little cherry?"

Zorg was turning blue.

Picasso, to whom blue was a sign of affection, was turning green with happiness.

"The truth is, my son, that life is a blessing," said Father Cornelius. "A precious gift, given with love—as I now give it to you."

Cornelius whacked Zorg on the back.

The cherry flew out of his mouth, striking Picasso between his beady eyes.

Zorg sat up, dazed. He looked around and pressed a button on the desktop console.

The office door slid open.

"You saved my life," Zorg said to Cornelius. "So I'm going to spare yours—for now. Guards!"

Two armed guards rushed into the room. Right Arm was right behind them.

"Throw him out!" said Zorg.

"You are a monster, Zorg," said Cornelius as the two guards dragged him from the room.

Zorg seemed finally to have regained his composure. "Thank you," he said. "I know."

He saw his secretary at the reception desk, doing her nails. She nodded at the priest being dragged from the room toward the elevator.

"Have a nice day, Father," she said, as the

office door slid shut and the elevator door slid open.

Zorg opened the cage door and took out Picasso and held him in his arms.

Right Arm stood quietly, waiting for the orders he knew would be coming sooner or later.

"Torture whoever you want," Zorg said. "The President, if you have to. But I want those stones."

Right Arm nodded.

"You have one hour."

Right Arm nodded and left the office.

Zorg sat for a long time, petting his monster and watching the sun set over the vast and troubled city.

# 15

LIGHT YEARS AWAY FROM ZORG AND HIS PET, THREE WARSHIPS
were positioned in front of a dark shape that had
congealed into a planet.

The warships were the cream of the United
Federation fleet. The best of the best.

The planet was the worst of the worst—a dark
conglomeration of an intelligent, or at least respon-
sive, anti-matter. It seemed to literally eat light,
leaving a null darkness from which the eye could
not be averted.

Small bright specks were being drawn into it.

One winked in from a far distance and disappeared. Then another, from another sector of the
galaxy.

They were drawn to its darkness as bugs are drawn
to light. It was an anti-light, a vacuum that sucked in
information, a black hole that ate technology.

"It's gobbling up all the communications satellites in the galaxy!" exclaimed a voice from one of
the watching ships.

Thanks to the magic of FTL (faster-than-light) plasma optics, the dark planet also appeared on a viewscreen in an office in Manhattan.

The voice from the ship was heard there too.

The listener was a large black man slumped over in a chair bearing the seal of the United Federation.

The President.

"Why the hell is it eating up all those satellites?" he asked.

A grim-faced scientist stood at his elbow.

"We're working on it, President Lindberg."

"It should only choke on them," groaned the President.

General Munro entered the office as the scientist left.

Also entering the office was a small cockroach—or what appeared to be a cockroach. The tiny antennae on its back revealed it to be a genetically altered biological (GAB) listening device.

Connected to the scurrying GAB was a man in a small room across town, listening on earphones.

Right Arm.

General Munro saluted the President. "I managed to contact the Mondoshawans," he said. "They deplore the incident, but accept our apologies."

The President breathed a sigh of relief. "And the stones? Did you find them in the wreckage of the Mondoshawan ship?"

"The Sacred Stones weren't aboard the ship."

---

"What?" The President was all ears.

So, thanks to the magic of nanotech, was Right Arm.

"The Mondoshawans never fully trusted the human race," said General Munro. "So they gave the stones to someone they do trust. Her name is Plavalaguna."

"Plavalawho?"

"Plavalaguna," said Munro. "She's a famous diva, and she's going to sing at the charity ball on Fhloston Paradise in a few hours. She has the Sacred Stones with her."

"Excellent," said the President, taking off one shoe.

*Excellent!* breathed Right Arm to himself.

"Damn bugs!" said the President. He smashed the cockroach on his desk.

WHACK!

And Right Arm's earphones flew off.

Thanks to the magic of audio amplification.

"I want this operation to be as discreet as possible," said the President. "No troops, no big operation. The council doesn't have to know about this yet. I want your best man on this."

"Hmmmm," said Munro. "I have the perfect man."

Munro's perfect man was throwing up into his toilet bowl.

His cat looked on through the open bathroom door. People had the strangest habits. But hair balls?

From the window, the Thai cook looked on

with professional concern. He was holding the remains of the dessert. It was a special delicacy made with live squid, honey still in the bees, and sweetened jellyfish excrement.

"You no like the dessert?"

Korben gave a weak thumbs up. "I just ate it too fast," he said. "I guess."

The phone rang.

Korben picked it up. "Hello?"

"You are the nastiest dirtbag I know in this stinking city!"

"Hi, Ma," said Korben.

He held the receiver a few inches from his ear.

"I've been playing twice a week for twenty years! Twenty years I've been eating those shitty croquettes!"

Korben crossed the room and found a cigarette.

"You wouldn't even eat one to help your poor mother, and you win the big prize? Know something? The whole thing makes me sick!"

"I can relate, Ma," said Korben, even though he had no idea what she was talking about.

He searched the pockets of his vest for a match. Meanwhile, at the window, the Thai Fly By was starting to clean up.

Korben covered the receiver. "Go ahead. This could take a while."

"I leave it here," said the cook. "Go ahead, take your time."

He put the dessert on the windowsill and cast off with a wave.

The dessert was still moving. From inside the crust, Korben could hear tiny screams.

"Are you still listening, you ingrate?"

"Yes, Ma," said Korben, sitting down at his table. "Other than that, you all right?"

He tried a match.

No luck.

"And now you're making fun of me. I'm warning you!"

Korben tried the second match.

It lit.

"If you don't take me after all those years of sacrifice, I'll never forgive you!"

"Ma, what are you talking about?"

"I get it. You want to make me beg, is that it?"

"All I want is an explanation," Korben said. "I just got in, I lost my job, I smashed my cab. I got mugged, but other than that everything's peachy, Ma. Thanks for asking. Now settle down and explain to me what you are talking about. Ooow!"

The forgotten second match burned Korben's hand.

He dropped it and it went out.

"You just won a trip, you dolt! Ten days in Fhloston Paradise for two!"

"Ma, if I had won, I would know about it. Someone would have notified me."

"Meow."

The cat was looking at the message tube. The "incoming" light was blinking.

Korben took out his last match. One more try.

"They've been blaring out your name on the radio for the last hour, blockhead!"

Korben looked at the message waiting in the tube. He was just about to reach for it when—

BBRRRIIINNGGG!

The doorbell rang.

Korben put his last match back in the match-box.

"Ma, it's the door. Wait a second . . ."

He clicked HOLD and turned on the hallway security monitor.

He saw a familiar face. Too familiar.

He clicked the phone back on. "Mother, I'll call you back."

He opened the door.

"Nice apartment, Major," said General Munro, entering without waiting to be invited in.

Behind him was a woman in uniform. A sort of a woman. All she needed to be a man was a moustache.

"Looks like you've settled into a wonderful life since leaving the service," said Munro. "Except I hear you've lost your job."

Korben's arms were folded. "I'll find another one."

"Don't bother," said Munro. "We have a job for you."

"Nice to see you're still thinking of me," said Korben.

"More than ever," said Munro. He snapped his fingers and the female officer opened a file and handed him a sheet of paper.

"Major Korben Dallas," Munro read in his best clipped and pressed military tones. "You have just been selected for a mission of the utmost importance."

"What mission?"

"To save the world," said Munro.

"I was afraid of that," said Korben. "I think I've heard this song before."

Munro ignored him. "You are to leave immediately for Fhloston Paradise. Retrieve four stones from the Diva Plavalaguna. And bring them back with the utmost discretion possible."

Munro handed the paper back to the female officer, who put it back into the file.

"Any questions?"

"Just one," said Korben. "Why me? I'm retired, six months already. Remember?"

"Three reasons," said General Munro. "One— as a member of the Elite Special Forces unit of the United Federation armed forces, you are an expert in the use of all weapons and spacecraft needed for this mission.

"Two—of all the members of your unit you were the most decorated."

Korben remained unconvinced. "And the third one?"

"You're the only one left alive."

Before Korben could respond, Munro bent over

the flashing tube and took out the incoming communication. It was two tickets wrapped in a message. "Don't you bother to open your incoming?"

"I've had enough good news for today," said Korben.

"You have won the annual Gemini Croquettes contest, and a trip to Fhloston Paradise," said Munro, without reading the message. "For two. Congratulations."

He handed the tickets to Korben, who looked at them, and then back at the general.

"You rigged the contest?"

General Munro nodded.

"You couldn't come up with something a little more—discreet?"

Munro shook his head. "Old tricks are the best tricks," he said.

He stepped back and the female officer stepped forward. "Major Iceborg here will accompany you, as your wife."

Korben was already shaking his head. "I'm not going."

"Why not?" asked Munro.

"One reason," said Korben. "I want to remain the only one from my unit left alive."

# 16

**THE HALLWAY WAS DARK.**

Strange insects scurried out of sight, as Leeloo and Father Cornelius searched for Korben's apartment.

Leeloo carried the cheap flashing business card Korben had given her.

She studied each door, and then the card, with all the intensity of a child learning a new language.

*Match!*

She held the business card next to Korben's nameplate on the door, and was just about to knock (a universal sign meaning 'request entry') when Father Cornelius stopped her hand.

She looked at him inquisitively. "Asin get let deloun omekta?"

Cornelius carefully peeled Korben's nameplate off his apartment door.

"Your friend won the last two tickets available," he said. "I can assure you we are not the only people with the idea of contacting him."

---

120

He handed the nameplate to Leeloo. "Stick it on another door—down the hall."

Korben's doorbell rang.

"'Scuse me," he said to General Munro and Major Iceborg.

Looking through the peephole he saw what he first thought was a fantasy, and then a vision from heaven. It was her!

Leeloo.

The most gorgeous girl in the world—at his door!

Korben started to fling the door open.

Then he remembered General Munro and Major Whatsername.

"Shit!" he muttered under his breath.

"What is it?" Munro asked, worried. "Is something wrong?"

"It's uh . . ." Korben fumbled for a handy lie. How could he get rid of these two? Something told him he did *not* want Leeloo mized up with the military.

"It's my wife!" he blurted out.

"You're remarried?" Munro asked.

Iceborg looked on icily.

"No," said Korben. "I mean, yes. I mean, soon. It's a brand new thing. You can't stay here!"

"Why not?" Munro asked.

"She hates everything in a uniform," said Korben. "If she sees you guys here, it's all over.

Please! You made my first marriage hell. Don't screw this one up before it starts. In here . . ."

He punched a wall button. A conveyer hummed as his shower was replaced by a walk-in freezer.

Taking Munro with one hand and Iceborg with the other, Korben herded them toward the freezer.

"Major," said Munro, "we have no time for this!"

"A minute!" said Korben, opening the freezer door. "It'll take a minute. I'll set up another meeting with her."

He shoved them both into the vaultlike freezer.

"Be right with you!" he called out to Leeloo.

He jammed the half-eaten jellyfish cake into Munro's hands. "Don't eat it!" he warned, and before the general could protest, he slammed the door.

"Coming!"

A mess! The prettiest girl in the galaxy was at the door, and the place was a mess! Korben's long dormant hormones raged through his body, and he saw his apartment through Leeloo's perfect green eyes.

Disgusting!

He swept the dirty dishes off the table and into the trash (which groaned with faux-biological satisfaction). He rolled his dirty clothes up into a ball, and shut them up in the folding bed.

Whipping a comb out of his vest pocket, he ran it through his thinning hair.

Then with a smile of anticipation, he opened the apartment door—

And looked straight down the barrel of a gun held by Father Cornelius.

Korben hardly noticed. He only had eyes for Leeloo, who was standing behind the priest.

"Apipoulai!" she said.

"I suppose that means *Hi*," said Korben.

Cornelius pulled Leeloo into the apartment, and Korben shut the door behind them.

"I'm sorry we have to resort to such methods," said Cornelius, waving the gun menacingly. "But we heard about your good luck on the radio, and we need the tickets to Fhloston Paradise."

"Is this the usual way priests go on vacation?" asked Korben, in what he hoped was a voice dripping with scorn and irony.

"We're not going on vacation," said Cornelius. "We're on a mission."

"What kind of mission?"

"We have to save the world," said Cornelius.

Korben sat down at the table and laughed. "Is there an echo in here?"

Cornelius looked at him, uncomprehending.

"Oh, no," said Korben sarcastically. "I get it. It's Tuesday, right? Tuesday must be save-the-world day. So tell me, Father, are you going to save the world all by yourself?"

"Well, of course," said Father Cornelius with unaffected sincerity. "But if you want to help, we would be thrilled."

Leeloo smiled her agreement.

Korben didn't notice. He was too busy shaking his head *no no no*, and pointing his thumbs *down down down*!

"Father," he said, "I was in the army for a while, and every time they told us we were on a mission to save the world, the only thing that changed was that I lost a lot of friends. So thanks for the offer—but no thanks."

Cornelius looked disappointed. Leeloo, standing right next to him, looked absolutely devastated.

Her radiant smile was gone.

Korben saw the disappointment in her wide green eyes, and was just about to reconsider, when the silence was broken by an amplified robotic voice from outside the window.

"THIS.IS.A.POLICE.CONTROL.ACTION."

Father Cornelius backed up against the wall, panicked, the gun in his hand forgotten.

Korben took the gun from his hand and went to the door. He looked through the peephole.

The hallway was swarming with cops.

A squad was standing on the landing, armed with lights, crowd control bungees, shields, helmets, and laser rays that could see through every door into every apartment.

"Oh my god," said Cornelius. "Do you think they're after us?"

"Let's not find out," said Korben. He pushed the wall button again, sending the walk-in freezer to the next floor, and returning the shower in its place.

"Leeloo," he said, "hide in there, and don't move!"

Without hesitation, she jumped into the shower. The door closed behind her.

Korben opened the folding bed.

"What are you doing?" Cornelius demanded.

"Trying to save your ass," said Korben, shoving the priest onto the bed, into the pile of dirty laundry. "So you can save the world!"

He pressed the button that sent the bed back into the wall. He grabbed the two tickets off the table and slid them into his belt—

SPLAT!

Just as a transparent circle suddenly appeared on the apartment door, where the cops had slapped on a *see-thru* sticker.

"SPREAD.YOUR.LEGS.AND.PLACE.YOUR. HANDS.IN.THE.YELLOW CIRCLES," said a robotic cop voice.

Splat! Splat!

Two smaller circles appeared on the door. These were laser holding devices.

PLACE.YOUR.HANDS.IN.THE.YELLOW. CIRCLES.PLEASE!

A cop was peering through the *see-thru*. He was holding a Wanted sheet with Korben's picture on it. It was an old military picture, showing Korben with long hair and a beard.

HANDS.IN.THE.YELLOW.CIRCLES.NOW!

Korben moved slowly toward the door, keeping his face turned away as much as possible.

"Are you human?" asked the cop, straining to get a better view.

"No," said Korben. "I'm a meat popsicle."

The cop was just about to examine Korben's face up close when a voice came from down the hall.

"I found him!"

The nameplate on the door said Korben Dallas.

Bingo!

The cop stuck a *see-thru* sticker on the door.

Korben's nasty neightbor was shaving. His face was covered with shaving cream. Almost like a beard.

The cop turned off his robotic bullhorn. Why make a big fuss and annoy everybody?

"This is a control," he said politely. "Please put your hands in the yellow circles."

Korben's nasty neighbor peered through the transparent circle on his door.

He saw two young cops, nervously holding stun guns and a picture of a guy with a beard.

They saw a guy shaving.

"Open the door!" they said

Never at a loss for a response, the nasty neighbor said what he always said when faced with a new irritant in an always irritating world:

"Fuck you!"

Korben heard it all from his own apartment.

He heard the police request and the nasty neighbor's answer.

Then he heard the blasting of the door, the stun gun shots, the struggle.

He smiled. "Wrong answer."

There were more footsteps, and more cops came running.

Korben watched through the *see-thru*, which was already fading back to opacity.

He saw the cops dragging the squirming arrest bag down the hall, manhandling it down the stairwell.

"Okay, okay! " one of them was hollering down to the street. "We got the guy under wraps!"


Right Arm also heard it all.

He was on the phone in Zorg's office, patched into the police lines via cell phone.

"It wasn't easy, but we bagged him," a police lieutenant said over the phone. "Thanks for the tip."

"Glad to help," said Right Arm. He smiled as he hung up the phone.

"They just arrested this Dallas character for uranium smuggling," he said proudly to Zorg. "Everything's going as I planned."

"Uranium smuggling?" Zorg was skeptical. "I thought he was wanted on traffic violations and evading arrest?"

"A clerical error," Right Arm said. "I patched it into the allpoints code just to make sure."

He showed Zorg a forged plane ticket and passport—both in the name of Korben Dallas.

"All I have to do now is go to the spaceport and take his place. I should be on Fhloston in less than four hours."

Zorg was unimpressed. "Don't come back without the stones."

# 17

KORBEN OPENED THE SHOWER. LEELOO WAS STANDING UNDER the spray, shivering violently.

"I'm sorry," said Korben. "I forgot the hot water doesn't work too well in this old racktower."

He dragged a blanket out of a corner and wrapped her in it.

She snuggled into his arms, still shivering violently.

Korben's rubbing slowed, passing gradually over the line that divides a friendly rub from an intimate caress.

"It's funny," he said. "I've met you twice today, and you've ended up in my arms both times."

Leeloo smiled and snuggled even closer. "Vallo massa. Chacha hamas."

"Uh . . . you're welcome," said Korben.

Nervously, he pulled away.

"Coffee! That's what you need," he said. He hit the control pad on the microwave.

*Such eyes!* They made him nervous. "A nice hot cup of coffee. With honey."

He had sworn off women for good. Hadn't he?

So why was his heart pounding?

"With honey!" Korben said agitatedly. "You'll see, honey's great!"

But where was the damn honey? Korben opened drawer after drawer, rummaging through six months of unsorted bachelor debris.

"A hot cup of coffee . . . with honey . . ."

Leeloo seemed to want to help. Still wrapped in the army blanket, she followed him around the tiny apartment, opening and shutting drawers.

"Huh knee!" she said.

"I've got this great honey somewhere," Korben babbled nervously. "You know about honey? There used to be these little animals with antennae who made it . . ."

Leeloo found a picture in one of the drawers. She took it out and held it up.

It was Major Korben Dallas, War Hero. Accepting a medal for Valor Above and Beyond.

". . . and there were these other animals that ate it," Korben went on. "Some were called bees and some were called bears."

Leeloo looked from the War Hero to the nervous, fumbling man who was babbling to her about bears and bees . . .

And she smiled.

"I forget which ate it and which made it," said Korben. "But . . . here it is!"

He held up an old-fashioned screw-top jar. He unscrewed the top.

"Taste this."

Leeloo stuck her lovely finger into the pot of honey; then stuck the same finger into her lovely mouth.

Korben was mesmerized.

"It . . . melts in your mouth, uh, doesn't it?"

Leeloo nodded. She sucked her finger sensually; then dipped all four slender fingertips into the jar, and sucked them clean . . . one by one by one by . . .

Korben was lost.

Gone.

Helpless.

He was so enthralled by the sight of Leeloo that he didn't even hear the muffled knocking from inside the wall.

Until it became a steady thud.

Thump.

Thump!

THUMP!

**THUMP !!!**

"Do you hear that?" Korben asked.

Leeloo nodded, still licking her fingertips.

"Cor knee lee us," she said.

"Oh, God!"

Korben pushed the button on the wall, and the bed popped open.

Father Cornelius was tangled in the dirty laundry, upside down.

"I'm really sorry," Korben said. "Let me help you!"

"We don't need your help," said Cornelius, untangling himself up with all the dignity he could muster.

*Bleep!* went the microwave.

"Coffee's ready," said Korben. He crossed to the counter and poured a cup for himself and one for Leeloo.

"I'm warning you," he said. "Coffee's not my specialty."

He turned to offer her her cup—and saw that she had removed her wet clothing. She was wringing them into the sink.

She had set aside the army blanket.

She was nude.

Shockingly, fetchingly, adorably, magnificently, wonderfully and totally nude.

Perfectly nude.

Embarrassed, Korben turned away, back toward the coffeepot.

"Maybe I should, uh, keep it hot," he muttered. "I like it . . . hot."

Behind him, Cornelius was studying a heavy, dusty military trophy—an award Korben had gotten during a forgotten war and now used as a paperweight.

Cornelius hefted it, then raised it over his head—and brought it down on the back of Korben's head.

A short, sharp shock.

Leeloo looked at Cornelius angrily. "Vano da, mechtaba? Soun domo kala chon hammas!"

"I know," said Cornelius. "I'm not proud of myself. But we don't have the luxury of choice."

Meanwhile, the police SWAT team was taking the bagged nasty neighbor out the entrance to a waiting cruiser, when they, too, felt a short, sharp shock.

Pop!

Pop!

Pop!

Three tranq shots from silenced weapons, and the cops folded up like newspaper in the rain.

Three Mangalore warriors, experienced shapeshifters, picked up the body bag even as their features were shifting back to their natural, hideous form. The strain of looking human had taken its toll, and all three warriors were exhausted.

They hauled the body into the back of a hovering van, where Aknot, still alive but seriously injured from the warehouse blast, was waiting impatiently.

"Korben Dallas," the Mangalore hit team leader said, indicating the squirming bag. "We got him!"

"Perfect," groaned Aknot. "Take command, Akanit. Go to Fhloston and get the stones. If Zorg really wants them, he'll have to negotiate."

He closed his narrow eyes.

"Revenge is at hand!"

Korben struggled to his feet.

He looked around the apartment, which had only just recently been graced with the beautiful image and presence of Leeloo.

And that grim priest.

Both gone.

"Jesus!" said Korben. He put a hand to the back of his head. It was sticky with blood.

The plot thickened.

BRRRRIIIINNNNG!

Korben picked up the phone with one hand, while he kept the other on the back of his head.

"Yeah?"

"Have you pulled yourself together yet!?!"

"Not yet, Ma."

He hung up.

Korben's head was killing him. He needed ice.

He pressed the wall button and the conveyer groaned, replacing the shower with the walk-in freezer.

He opened the door and faced the frozen stares of General Munro and Major Iceborg.

Whoops! Forgot.

"I'll accept the mission," Korben said, grabbing a few cubes and closing the door.

# 18

MANHATTAN INTERGALACTIC AIRPORT WAS ALMOST FULL.

Of trash, not travelers.

A strike was in progress, and the sanitation workers had let the garbage pile up almost to the ceiling of the lobby.

Narrow paths bulldozed through the debris led to the check-in counters and terminal gates.

Striking workers marched and chanted. Some were human, some were 'bots or 'droids; others were alien or altered. They all carried picket signs.

The police, meanwhile, were massing to move in. The air was thick with tension, like the electricity before a summer storm.

The novice, David, was watching when he felt a hand on his shoulder.

"Yaahhh!" he cried, jumping back.

He turned and saw Father Cornelius and the lovely Leeloo, still dripping wet—but fully dressed.

"Did you get them?" asked Cornelius, never a man to beat around the bush.

David nodded. He handed the priest two passports.

"Excellent," said Cornelius, opening them and studying the forgery work.

He handed one to Leeloo. "Leeloo Dallas."

She smiled delightedly and took it.

"And Korben David Dallas. Perfect!" Father Cornelius handed the second passport back to David.

Leeloo's smile faded. "Akta dedero ansila deno poerfect?"

Father Cornelius shook his head. "Leeloo, I can't pretend to be your husband. I'm old. David's in great shape. He's young, he's strong. He'll protect you."

David seemed to swell up with each syllable of praise. He held out a hand toward Leeloo, who took it somewhat reluctantly.

*Bam!*

*Bam!*

Father Cornelius looked around nervously toward the strikers as the cops moved in and shots were fired. He pointed toward the line at the check-in counter.

"Go on! See the Diva, get the Sacred Stones. I will wait for you at the Temple. God be with you!"

*Bam!*

*Whang!*

Korben ducked as a wild shot shattered the glass behind his head. He dodged and weaved as he ran across the trash-filled airport lobby.

He scanned the crowd, looking for Leeloo.

All he could see were strikers, diving head first into the garbage piles to avoid the charging police.

The gate sign was flashing: "Fhloston Non-Stop, First Boarding Call."

Casually brushing off two policemen who had mistaken him for a striker, Korben picked his way through the garbage toward the check-in counter.

"Congratulations," said the check-in attendant.

David looked confused.

"On winning the Gemini Croquette contest— the trip to Fhloston Paradise!" the attendant said, as she stapled the boarding pass to David's ticket and handed him back his passport.

"Oh, yeah," he said.

"I made it!" Korben said. He jammed his knuckles into David's back like a gun, and snatched the passport out of his hand.

"I really thought I was going to miss my flight," he added to the confused attendant.

Leeloo's face broke into a wide smile.

"Thanks, kid," Korben said, hustling David to one side. "You put the luggage on the conveyer belt?"

He poked him convincingly with the "gun."

"Uh, yeah," David said haltingly.

"Great!" said Korben, giving David a playful but effective shove into the garbage pile. "Now beat it!"

Korben turned his most charming smile on the confused check-in attendant. "I was so afraid I would miss my flight that I sent the kid here to pick up my boarding pass."

Leeloo smiled, and held out her hand for her own ticket.

The attendant held back Leeloo's boarding pass and passport. She looked at them suspiciously.

"Your wife?" she asked Korben.

Korben grabbed the passport and read it. "Uh, yes," he said. "Newlyweds. Love at first sight. You meet, something goes 'tilt,' you get married, you hardly know each other. Right, darling?"

Leeloo reached across the counter and grabbed her boarding pass from the attendant.

"Dinoine chagatakat!"

"Took the words right out of my mouth, sweetie. Go on, I'll be right with you."

Korben turned back to the attendant.

"It's our honeymoon," he said with a broad wink. "She's nervous."


A familiar nasty face was entering the front door of the airport, clambering over and through the festering garbage.

It was the face of Korben's nasty neighbor,

accompanied by a young woman with a curiously blank expression.

As the two picked their way through the garbage, they were almost knocked over by a huge pink beast—

A police pig, on a steel chain leash.

"Come on Snyffer, go root!" said a pork-patrol handler, running along behind the pig.

The nasty neighbor stepped aside, then pushed on toward the check-in counter.

The blank-faced girl followed.

A few feet away, Father Cornelius watched from a stool at the Take-off Bar, nursing his second martini.

"I feel so guilty," he said to the robot bartender. "Sending Leeloo to do the dirty work—like these poor police pigs. I know she was made to be strong, but she seems so fragile. So human. Know what I mean?"

The bartender had a monitor for a face. It glowed with compassion and nodded gravely.

Robots are good listeners.

The nasty neighbor handed his ticket to the check-in attendant.

She looked at him, surprised.

"Dallas? Korben Dallas?"

"Yes," said the nasty neighbor. "That's me."

The attendant smiled politely. Meanwhile, her foot tripped a switch that turned on an overhead ultralight passenger scanner.

The ultralight revealed that the nasty neighbor and his blank-faced girlfriend were both Mangalores.

The attendant never blew her cool, however.

"Just a moment, please," she said in her sweetest the-customer-is-always-right voice.

With her other foot she tripped a silent alarm.

Sensing trouble, the Mangalores both backed away.

"We'll be right back!" said the nasty neighbor suspiciously. He grabbed his 'girlfriend' by the hand and dragged her away, into the crowd.

"The same?" asked the robot bartender.

Father Cornelius's eyes were glazed over. "Yeah."

"Make that two," said a voice at his elbow.

Cornelius was surprised to see the novice, David, seated on the stool next to him.

He sobered up real fast. "Where's Leeloo?" he asked in a horrified whisper.

David swallowed his martini and slammed the glass down on the bar, cowboy style.

The stem snapped.

"On the flight. With Mr. Dallas. The real one."

"What?"

"He put a gun right here," said David. He

turned on his stool and showed Cornelius the small of his back.

"Oh, my Lord!" said Father Cornelius. "This is all my fault. I'm the servant; it was my mission. I should never have given it to you."

David was already ordering his second martini.

Father Cornelius reached under his cassock and snapped the chain around his neck.

He handed the crooked steel finger to David. "Here!"

"Huh?"

"The key to the temple," said Cornelius as he tossed down David's martini, and then his own. "Go and prepare for our arrival. I go to face my destiny!"

And he was gone, into the milling crowd.

Unfortunately, he was right behind the Mangalore, whose nasty-neighbor face was flickering in and out of focus as he and the "girl" ran, faster and faster, toward the airport exit.

"Tell Aknot that plan A flopped," the neighbor Mangalore said to the girl Mangalore. "Go to plan B."

She nodded and peeled off, jumping over the garbage toward the exit.

Two cops stepped in front of the neighbor Mangalore.

He drew his ZF1 and fired twice, then dove into the pile.

*Bratabrat!*

*Bratabrat!*

The cops fired back.

---

141

*Bam!*

*Bam!*

"Send a backup!" one cop yelled into his walkie talkie. "Zone 7!"

Cornelius was backed against the wall, trying to avoid the flying bullets.

A trap door opened in the wall behind him, and three gigantic pigs rushed out, followed by their armored pork-patrol handlers.

The trap door bobbed up and down, then started to close.

Cornelius looked right, then left—

Then got down on all fours and crawled through the trap door, just before it closed.

"Excuse me!" said Korben.

He was being led by a stewardess down a long hall in the first class lounge.

She had insisted that Korben come with her. Her high heels went *click click click* and she walked so fast that he could barely keep up.

"I shouldn't leave my wife alone," protested Korben. "My wife—when she's nervous, she's . . ."

He searched for the word to describe Leeloo; then found it:

". . . unpredictable!"

"This will only take a minute," the stewardess said. "Loc Rhod is the quickest DJ in the universe. You are SO lucky!"

Korben was not so sure.

"Listen," he said, "I'm sure he's very cool, but I don't want to be interviewed. I'd really prefer to remain anonymous."

The stewardess stopped and turned to face Korben.

"Forget anonymous!" she said. "You'll be doing Loc Rhod's live show every day from five to seven."

Korben was beginning to perceive the magnitude of the public relations circus to which he had, unwittingly, attached himself. "You've got to be kidding," he said, even as he was realizing that she not only didn't have to be, but wasn't.

The stewardess smiled and shook her head.

Not kidding.

WHAP!

A door opened, knocking a few new stars in the already sore heaven of Korben's consciousness.

Through the door came a being of intense vivacity, impeccable sartorial integrity, and intermittent intelligibility.

A young black man with an elaborate "do," velvet bell bottoms and boat-sized pointed-toed shoes.

The 24th century's most popular DJ.

Loc Rhod.

"Korben Dallas!!" said the DJ, speaking into a mike that doubled as a silver cane, in a rhythmic voice that sounded more like rap than radio reportage. "Here he is!! The one and only winner of the Gemini Croquettes contest!!"

Loc Rhod turned to scan the crowd that was already gathering around him.

"This boy is fueled like fire!! Ladies, start melting because he is hot, *hot*, HOT!!"

Loc Rhod put his hand on Korben's arm.

"Right size!!" he said. "Right build, right hair, right on!! And he's ready to say something to those fifty billion eager ears out there!! Pop it, D-Man!!"

He stuck the mike in Korben's face.

"Uh . . . hi!" said Korben.

Loc Rhod winced and pulled back his silver rhinestone-studded mike. "Un Be Leave A Bull!!" he said.

He grabbed Korben's arm and led him down the hallway.

The crowd fell in behind them.

"Quiver, ladies, quiver!!" crooned Loc Rhod. "He's gonna set the world on fire, right here from five to seven!! You'll know everything there is to know 'bout the D-Man!! His dreams, his desires, his most intimate of intimates!! And from what I'm looking at, *intimate* is this stud muffin's middle name!!"

He bent down and put the mike in Korben's face again.

"So tell me, my main man, you nervous in the service??"

"Uh . . . not really," stammered Korben.

Loc Rhod put his arm around the stewardess.

"Freeze those knees, my chickadees, cause Korben is on the case with a major face!!"

The procession paused at an intersection in the

corridor, where the airline's catering service had placed a robot with a tray of champagne glasses.

Loc Rhod grabbed a glass, drained it, tossed it away; all the while scribbling autographs as he rapped nonstop:

"Yesterday's frog will be tomorrow's Prince of Fhloston Paradise!!"

An aide handed him a cue card.

"The hovering hotel of a thousand and one follies, dollies, and lickin' lollies!! A magic fountain flowing with nonstop wine, women and hootchie koothchie koo!! All night long, ooowwwooooo!!"

Korben looked on amazed, as the smooth and supple DJ grabbed two stewardesses by the arm, and continued rapping as easily as others walk or breathe. It seemed to be an unconscious activity with him; the rhymes and rhythms flowed without thought as his eyes appraised the crowd that followed him everywhere he went.

"And start licking your stamps, little girls, this guy's gonna have you writin' home to momma!! Tomorrow from five to seven, I'll be your voice, your tongue, and I'll be hot on the trail of the sexiest man of the year!! D-man!! Your man!! My man!! . . ."

*Bleep.*

"End of transmission," said an engineer's voice over a distant speaker.

Loc Rhod stopped in his tracks.

The hallway fell silent.

Two assistants ran up to Loc Rhod, one with a cigarette, another with a match.

Loc Rhod lit the cigarette, blew out a cloud of dissolving smoke, and asked, "How was it?"

"Oh, green!" said one assistant.

"How green?"

"Oh green green green!" said another assistant. "Super green. Crystal green."

Loc Rhod approached Korben.

He put his hand on his arm, and in an oily, unctuous voice, said, "Korben, sweetheart, do me a favor . . ."

*Sweetheart*? Korben looked at the DJ skeptically. *Favor*?

"I know that this is probably the biggest thing that has ever happened to you in your inconsequential life," said Loc Rhod. "But I've got a show to do here and it's got to pop, pop, POP! So tomorrow, when we're on the air, give me a hand."

*A hand?* Korben stared unbelievingly at the arrogant little DJ.

"Try to make believe you have more than a six-word vocabulary. You green, pal?"

Instead of answering, Korben grabbed Loc Rhod by the collar.

A security guard stepped forward, but Korben shoved him out of the way. His partner hesitated.

Korben rammed Loc Rhod against the wall, wedging his head into the corner, holding him up so that his feet were six inches off the floor.

"*Green?*" Korben said. "I didn't come here to play Dumbo on the radio. So tomorrow between five and seven, give *yourself* a hand. You GREEN, pal?"

Loc Rhod's eyes were about to bulge out of his head. "Super green!" he said.

The check-in attendant, resplendent in her see-thru dress and vinyl pillbox hat, examined the two tickets in her hand.

She read them curiously.

"Mr. Dallas? Mr. Korben Dallas?"

"That's right," said Zorg's Right Arm, giving her his most persuasive smile.

Which was not very persuasive.

With her foot, the check-in attendant tripped the passenger scanner, and its ultralight beam played across the face of Zorg's Right Arm.

Which remained the face of Zorg's Right Arm.

"The problem is," said the attendant, "I have only one Korben Dallas on my list. And he's already checked in."

"Impossible!" said Right Arm, his smile shattering. "He's in jail—I mean, there must be some mistake. I have my ticket. And I am the *real* Korben Dallas!"

DING! A bell rang at the end of the gate corridor.

"Sorry, sir," said the attendant. "Boarding is finished."

Zorg's Right Arm reached for the attendant, just as a thick plexi screen rose from the check-in counter.

"I'm Korben Dallas!" Right Arm yelled, thinking of the torments Zorg would prepare for him if he failed. "I want to see your boss! Get rid of this stupid window! Somebody's made a mistake, goddammit!"

He pounded on the counter with both fists.

The only result was that a steel curtain descended to back up the plexi screen.

"THIS.IS.NOT.AN.EXERCISE!" said a robotic voice from an indeterminate spot in the air, where an atmospheric speaker node had temporarily coalesced.

Red laser sighting beams sliced through the air, forming target spots on Right Arm's body.

"THIS.IS.A.POLICE.CONTROL. PUT.YOUR.HANDS.IN.THE.YELLOW.CIRCLES."

Gun barrels protruded from the wall, the counter, the floor.

"Sorry!" said Right Arm, in his best dealing-with-insane-authority voice. "Just a little over-excited. That's all. I'm CALM now . . ."

# 19

Korben hated space travel.

The military ships were bad enough, with all the cannon fodder lined up in hard aluminum seats, each man lost in his own nervous thoughts as he was warped across the galaxy toward the latest suicide mission.

Commercial coach class was even worse. Standing room only, and a tiny bag of dry roasted peanuts unless the trip was over a hundred light years, in which case you got half a cold sandwich and a peanut-butter cookie.

But this trip was different. No cattle car, no peanuts. First class only.

"Leeloo," Korben whispered as he made his way toward the back of the spaceship.

The corridor was lined with small private cabinettes.

"Leeloo . . ."

As if in answer to his deepest wish and fondest

dream, a cabinette door slid open silently, and there she was—stretched out on a velvet cushion, studying a computer screen.

First class!

She flashed Korben a galactic-quality smile as he sat down beside her.

"Apipoulai!" said Leeloo.

The cabinette door slid shut, and she turned back to the characters scrolling past on the screen. The search engines were humming.

"Yeah, I know," said Korben nervously. "Leeloo, listen to me. Those tickets you borrowed—they're not mine. I mean, they are, but not for a vacation like everyone thinks."

Leeloo shrugged. Did she understand? Korben wondered. Sometimes she seemed to understand everything—and at other times nothing. All he knew for sure was that he was on a very dangerous mission, and he wanted to keep her out of the line of fire.

"I'm working for some very serious people," he said. "And if I didn't come here with you, you'd be in a shitload of trouble. I'd love to be on vacation with you—"

It felt so good to tell the truth!

"But not now! Now I've got to work. And Leeloo—I would love to work in peace. Understand?"

Seemingly in answer, Leeloo typed a four-letter word into the keyboard:

L-O-V-E.

"Yes!" said Korben. "But 'love' isn't the operative word here. 'Peace' is."

Leeloo typed in P-E-A-C-E.

"Peace," she parroted, repeating after Korben. "And love . . ."

The computer's search engines whined and brought up a picture of a 1960's style hippie in love beads, flashing a peace sign.

Korben sighed. He had read about the hippies. Anti-war. He was anti-war, too, but from the inside out, not the outside in.

"Bad example," he said, switching off the computer. "You know, you can't learn everything from a screen. Sometimes it's better to ask someone who has experience."

"Okay!" said Leeloo, nodding happily. "What is . . . *make love*?"

"Uh . . ."

Korben stared at Leeloo. Such a combination of innocence and experience. He had never hesitated in front of a woman before, but this woman was . . . different.

This woman was truly what he wanted, and therefore he was truly afraid for the first time.

"Know what?" Korben said, blushing beet red. "Maybe on that subject maybe you'd be better off asking the screen."

And he switched the computer back on.


Meanwhile, in the corridor, a disembodied robotic voice announced in soothing tones: "To.make. your.flight.as.short.and.agreeable.as.possible.our.

flight.attendants.are.switching.on.the.snooze.
regulators.which.will.encourage.sleep.during.the.
trip . . ."

A stewardess made her way along the corridor,
pushing a red button on top of each first class
flight cabinette.

And in the cockpit, the captain and the copilot
were completing their preparations for departure.

"826 passengers aboard and accounted for . . ."

"Roger, checking list for preflight . . ."


"Okay! Finished!" Leeloo said.

She was speaking English? Korben looked at her
in amazement.

"Finished what?"

"Learning languages." She switched off the
computer.

"You mean . . . English?"

She nodded. "All nine hundred!"

Korben was amazed. "You learned all nine hundred Earth languages in just five minutes?"

"Yes! Now it's your turn. I learned your languages; you have to learn mine."

"I know how to say 'hello,'" Korben said.
"Apipoulai."

Leeloo nodded happily.

"Teach me how to say 'good-bye,'" Korben
said. "That's all I need to know."

"Apipoussan!"

"Apipoussan?" Korben repeated tentatively.

Leeloo nodded. "Good! Do you know how we say 'make love?'"

"Uh . . ." Korben fumbled.

"Hoppi-hoppa," said Leeloo.

Korben's heart and his resolve were melting rapidly as he looked into the eyes of the most beautiful creature he had ever beheld.

"Help," he mumbled in a small voice to himself.

At that moment, the stewardess pressed the snooze regulator button on the top of Korben's cabinette, and checked another name off her list.

"Sweet dreams, Mr. Dallas," she said.

Korben, who was about to take Leeloo in his arms, fell into hers instead.

Instantly asleep.

At the other end of the corridor, another stewardess was having a problem.

The problem was the celebrity.

The stewardess was used to galactic celebrities. This was the first-class shuttle, after all.

But this was the most famous galactic supercelebrity she had ever met.

And the most insistent.

"Mr. Loc Rhod," she said, "you'll have to assume your individual position."

He pulled her into his cabinette and down onto his lap. "I don't want an individual position," he said. "I want all positions."

The stewardess pulled back.

But not too hard.

"We're going to take off soon, Mr. Rhod!"

Loc Rhod buried his nose in her hair. "I'm gonna take off right now!"

In the cockpit, the captain was flipping switches on a long row of identical switches.

*clikclikclikclikclikclikclikclikclikclik*

They fell before his finger like bowling pins at a tournament.

". . . axis authorization confirmed . . ." droned the copilot.

The head stewardess entered the cockpit.

"Zone 1. Snooze regulators operative," she said.

The captain checked out her cute little see-thru suit.

"Roger that," he said.

She left with a smile.

Suddenly a green light flashed on the control panel.

"Alert the ground," said the copilot.

"There's a problem?" asked the captain impatiently. He was busy watching the stewardess's elegant departure.

"We've got parasites in the landing gear."

Moments later, on the ground, a truck pulled up under the massive underbelly of the galactic shuttle.

Two men in hi-tech, lo-risk hermetically sealed disinfectant suits got out.

They uncoiled a hose and sent a bright beam of cleansing fire up into the shuttle's wheel well.

Screams were heard. High piched screams, low pitched groans, curses, cries, exclamations and imprecations. A rain of hideous creatures dropped from the well, falling onto the stained tarmac.

While the disinfectant crew was vacuuming the still twitching parasites into the morguetank on the truck, another truck pulled up.

Two men climbed out and opened a trapdoor under the shuttle.

A phosphorescent tube as big as a log fell out.

"Yeah, it's me," said Right Arm. "Put Zorg on."

Right Arm was standing in the airport lobby, using one of the mobile phone booths that wandered around looking for customers.

"I'm listening," said Zorg coldly.

"The real Korben Dallas is on the plane!" said Right Arm. "He took my place!"

Zorg's voice was as cold as midwinter midnight. "This is a joke, right?"

Loc Rhod's arms and legs were wrapped around the stewardess as his hands explored her erogenous zones.

"No!" he whispered in her ear. "I swear to God. I've never been this sincere . . ."

The stewardess wavered. He was, after all, more than famous. He was superfamous.

". . . with a human before," Loc Rhod finished. "Really?"

"I'm fueled with sincerity," said Loc Rhod as his hips began to thrust forward urgently.

Two ground crew members put away the dim phosphorescent tube.

Two others, one of them human, the other from an outer galaxy species, inserted a new, highly phosphorescent tube into the shuttle.

The long slow insertion stroke was almost sexual.

The spaceship seemed to groan with pleasure.

"Fueled and ready to go," said the ground crew leader into a wrist mike.

In the cockpit, the captain answered, "Thank you."

He turned to his copilot. "Ready for lift off?"

"No!" said the stewardess, still weakening.

"No?" Loc Rhod spat. This was not a word he was used to hearing.

"I mean . . . not yet! I'm not ready."

"Not ready?"

"I like to talk first."

Loc Rhod brightened. Talk first, talk later, talk during—it was all talk to him.

And he began to rap sweet nothings into the stewardess's ear, as he began to disassemble her uniform.

"I can't XZXZXXDSD hear you," Zorg said. "We have a BFGFGGXCCZX connection here."

The mobile pay phone was waiting patiently.

Right Arm looked around the garbage-filled lobby for another, but they were all in use.

"What's CXCXCXXZXZ number?" Zorg asked. "I'll call you right back."

Right Arm wiped the crud off the mobile pay phone's faceplate. "278–645–321," he read.

"I'll XZXZ you right back," said Zorg cheerfully.

Too damn cheerfully, Right Arm thought, with a sudden involuntary chill.

The disinfectant truck rolled off in one direction.

The fuel truck rolled off in the other.

A man in a cassock stepped out of the shadows where he had been waiting.

It was Father Cornelius. He looked up into the now disinfected wheel well.

Pausing for an instant, he prayed swiftly and silently. Then he climbed up the landing gear, into the wheel well, as swiftly and silently as a capuchin monkey.

☼    ☼    ☼

"Power pressure," said the copilot.

The captain knocked down another row of switches.

*clikclikclikclikclikclikclikclikclikclik*

"Primed."

The stewardess had six buttons on her blouse.

Loc Rhod made up a poem for each one.

Her brassiere had two hooks.

Each was a sonnet.

"Protection?" asked the captain.

A shield dropped into place around the shuttle's engines.

"Confirmed," said the copilot.

The stewardess's legs rose slowly into the air.

They spread wider and wider and . . .

Zorg punched in the phone number his right arm, Right Arm, had given him.

"278 . . ."

Just as the captain pulled back on the throttle.

"Ten seconds!"

"Power increase . . ."

Just as Right Arm fended off an angry phone customer. "Come on, come on . . ." he muttered.

Just as the stewardess dropped her shoes, one by one, and crooned, "I'm on my way . . ."

Just as Zorg punched in more numbers:

"645 . . ."

Just as the engines peaked:

RRRRRROOOOOAAAARRRRRRRRR!

And Loc Rhod began his climactic Byronic stanza.

And the shuttle lifted off.

And the stewardess likewise: "Yeeeessss!"

And Zorg, smiling demonically, punched in the final numbers:

"321 . . ."

BARRROOOOOM!

The mobile pay phone exploded.

Right Arm was no more.

Along with everyone and everything else that had been within sixty feet of the pay phone.


Zorg hung up and lit a cigar.

The stewardess's scream softened to a satisfied whisper.

In the cockpit, the copilot said, "Landing gear secure."

The captain locked in the autopilot and disabled the cockpit smoke detector.

"Let's light one up."

# 20

**FIRST CLASS! WHAT'S NOT TO LIKE?**

Particularly with the new FTL (Faster than Light) Warp-Hop-Fold&Jump drive, which uses the elasticity of stretched superstrings to pull both Space and Time into conveniently traversed, commercially viable trade and travel routes.

Certainly, Leeloo and Korben were enjoying their trip.

In Korben's first-class cabinette they slept soundly. Leeloo's little hand was cuddled comfortably in Korben's big one, just as the two of them were cuddled in the warm, safe passenger area of the quarter-mile-long intragalactic shuttle.

Across the galaxy, however, a malevolent force was waiting:

The Dark Planet.

The Ultimate Evil.

Lights flashed across its surface, like random electric storms.

Nearby (relatively) in the admiral's starship, a technician turned away from her view screen.

Her face showed a mixture of relief, anticipation . . . and terror.

"Sir, we're finally getting something!"


Across the galaxy in the other direction, the President was slumped at his desk.

A giant of a man, President Lindberg had, like Lincoln (an ancient leader of one of the constituent political entities of the United Federation), poor posture.

"It's sending out radio signals!" said one of the President's scientists, who was standing with the other scientists behind the line of generals.

The President groaned. "What the hell does it want with radio waves?"

"Maybe," the scientist said, "it wants to make a call."

The President and all the generals turned and looked at him in astonishment.


Zorg sat in his office at his teak desk.

He loved his desk.

The last teak tree on the planet had been cut down and sawed up to make his desk. That made it special.

Picasso sat (or slumped, or squatted, or whatever it is that whatever it was does) on the desk, purring contentedly.

(Or whatever.)

BBBRRRIIINNNNG! The phone rang.

Picasso growled. (Or whatever.)

Zorg activated the intercom.

"I told you, I don't want to be disturbed!"

"*Mister Shadow* on the line," said the receptionist, enunciating slowly.

Zorg got to his feet. Picasso tumbled (or whatever) to the floor.

Zorg picked up the phone with trembling hands.

"Zorg here."

The voice that came through was dim, weak, feeble, as if it came from the remotest reaches of Time and Space.

But it was no less impressive for all that.

"AM I DISTURBING YOU?"

"No! No! Not at all. Where are you?"

"NOT FAR NOW."

"Gr-great!" stammered Zorg.

"HOW's OUR DEAL COMING ALONG?"

"F-fine," Zorg stammered. "Just fine. I'll have the four stones you asked for anytime now. But it wasn't easy."

Silence on the line.

A black, slimy liquid began to ooze from the top of Zorg's head.

"MONEY IS OF NO IMPORTANCE," said

the voice on Zorg's line. "I WANT THE STONES."

"The stones will be here," Zorg said in terror. The black liquid was oozing from his skull, over his brow, down his narrow sunken cheeks. "I'll see to it personally!"

"I CAN'T WAIT TO BE AMONG YOU."

The line clicked.

Dead.

Instead of hanging up, Zorg stood motionless in the center of his palatial office.

The black liquid was slowly fading from his face.

Only his trembling hands showed his total terror.

Across the galaxy, the Dark Planet was suddenly lifeless.

Dead.

"We lost it," said the tech on the bridge of the Admiral's starship.

"We lost the signal," said the general who stood by his side, speaking by direct FTL link to the United Federation headquarters in Manhattan, New York, Earth.

"Shit!" said the President.

"Aaaarrrggghhh!" screamed (or whatever) Picasso as Zorg sat on him absentmindedly.

"Sorry."

Zorg hung up the phone. His hand was still shaking.

"We got something!" said General Munro, rushing excitedly into the President's office.

He was almost fully recovered from his sojourn in Korben's freezer. Only a few black frostbitten fingertips remained to be amputated.

"What do you have?"

"A location," said Munro. "The signal came here. The contact was on Earth. Somewhere in the northern hemisphere."

President Lindberg raised his huge eyebrows. The gesture was as impressive as the opening of a hangar door. "This—*thing*—knows someone on Earth? General, warn your man. He could have trouble. Tell him to keep his eyes open."

General Munro saluted, then rushed out.

Peace prevailed in First Class Cabinette #318 of the intragalactic shuttle starship, *Pride of Brooklyn*.

Korben was snoring gently.

Leeloo lay awake in his arms, watching him sleep. A flicker of what might have been love shone in her deep green eyes.

A kilometer ahead, in the cockpit, the captain clicked the last of a row of switches.

*klikklikklikklik!*

"Leaving light speed."

The starship shuddered only slightly.

More like a snuggle, really—back into the familiar, comforting arms of Newtonian space.

Light filled the cabinette.

Korben stirred but didn't wake.

Leeloo was awake but not stirring.

What was more beautiful—the face she turned on Korben? Or the turquoise, cloud-flecked planet seen through the window, toward which the shuttle was swiftly descending?

"Ladies and gentlemen," came the Head Stewardess's voice. "We have begun our final descent toward Fhloston Paradise. The local time is 3:28 P.M. The outside temperature is a constant 82 degrees Fahrenheit. We hope you enjoyed your flight today, and we hope to see you again soon."

In the corridor, stewardesses were pressing the wakeup buttons on the cabinettes, one by one.

In one cabinette, Loc Rhod and the stewardess awoke with a start and began straightening their clothes.

The stewardess was embarrassed, but only slightly. The man who had ravished her was, after all, one of the most famous supercelebrities in the galaxy.

"I wanted to tell you . . ." she began.

Loc Rhod silenced her with a finger to her lips.

Dropping his sunglasses over his eyes, he left the cabinette—and left the stewardess to her sighs.

Clouds whipped by the wings like half-acknowledged thoughts as the shuttle drifted down toward a turquoise sea.

Hovering a dozen yards above the water was the Fhloston Paradise, a great floating hotel, modeled after the cruise ships of the past.

The shuttle suddenly appeared tiny as it drew near the great resort liner—like a sardine approaching a whale.

The stewardess hit the button on top of Korben's cabinette, and he awoke.

He looked around.

Where was Leeloo?

He panicked.

The captain slid the shuttle into the receiving dock on the Phloston Paradise.

Airlocks equalized, and the two-story-high door opened.

The most eager of the shuttle's passengers were already gathered at the door, waiting. When the door opened, they flooded off into the broad decks of the most luxurious liner in the known universe, decorated and appointed to resemble the fabulous *Normandie* of twentieth-century Earth.

Near the front of the crowd was Leeloo.

"Excuse me."

At the back of the crowd was Korben Dallas.

"Pardon me!" Korben jostled, hustled, fumbled, wedged and squeezed his way through the crowd of eager vacationers, trying to get to the front of the line.

"Hey, dude! You can't just . . ."

"I'm trying to find my wife," Korben muttered. He pushed the complainer against the wall. "Sorry!"

At the end of the passageway, just inside the reception deck of the Fhloston Paradise, a phalanx of cops in full riot gear waited.

For what?

Leeloo saw them and stopped; she squeezed herself against the wall and let the crowd go by.

Meanwhile Korben had almost caught up with her.

A gorgeous topless hostess in a grass skirt dropped a lei around his neck.

"Welcome to Paradise," she said—and planted a kiss on his lips.

Korben's eyes rolled wildly as he tried to break away. Where was Leeloo?

Then he saw her.

A fat man in a sarong—also topless—was dropping a lei around Leeloo's neck.

He smiled and planted a wet kiss on her lips—

"A mistake," Korben whispered, as he saw the fat man straighten up suddenly.

He was still smiling, but his nose was spurting blood as he sank slowly to the floor.

"Never without permission," muttered Korben.

He pushed on through the crowd toward Leeloo, wiping the lipstick from his face.

But she was gone.

After decking the dude, Leeloo ducked around a corner and saw a door marked PERSONNEL ONLY.

She stopped and punched random numbers into the code lock.

Nothing happened.

Looking over her shoulder, she twisted the knob.

*Crack!*

She opened the door.

Oops.

Three cops sat on three toilets, reading mail-order catalogs.

They looked up at her.

Leeloo smiled and closed the door behind her.

Where was Leeloo?

Always pushing toward the front, Korben followed the crowd through a high arched door, into the reception deck of the Fhloston Paradise.

Suddenly behind him he heard a shriek, followed by a chorus of oohs and aaaahs!

It was Loc Rhod—and he was heading straight for Korben.

The crowd parted around him like the sea around the prow of a speedboat.

A talking speedboat.

"My main man!!" Loc Rhod said, grabbing Korben's arm. "Please don't leave me here alone!! My head is killing me and my adoring fans are going to tear me apart!! Get me outta here!!"

Korben pulled back—then took pity on the DJ.

"I'll take you to the bar," he said. "After that, you're on your own. Okay?"

"Oh, green!" said Loc Rhod, clutching Korben's arm as if it were a life preserver. "Do that!! You treat me right, man!! I need more friends like you!! So tell me all about yourself: your roots, your personal life, your childhood dreams!!"

"I don't think this is a good time," said Korben distractedly. He was still scanning the crowd for Leeloo.

"You got brothers and sisters??" asked Loc Rhod. "What about your daddy?? Tell me about your daddy!! What was he like?? Physically, I mean!! Big, I suppose??"

"Yeah, very big . . ." said Korben, standing on his tiptoes, still trying to see into every corner of the crowded deck.

No luck.

No Leeloo.

He dragged Loc Rhod toward the bar, and cleared a space for the two of them.

Loc Rhod was still babbling.

"I never had a dad!! Never saw him!! Never even heard him!! Fifty billion people hear me every day, and he doesn't hear me . . ."

"I understand," said Korben, placing his hand on Loc Rhod's shoulder. "You're at the bar. Ciao!"

Loc Rhod turned to thank Korben, who was already gone.

"How can he leave me like this!!"

A voice at his elbow interrupted the DJ's self-pitying reverie.

"Mr. Rhod! I'm the manager of the hotel. Welcome to Paradise! The Princess Aachen of Minas Japhet would like to share a drink with you."

Loc Rhod looked at the manager, uncomprehendingly. Then he looked down the bar to where the manager's finger was pointing.

He raised his sunglasses and saw a young woman in an impossibly brief dress with an improbably welcoming smile.

Loc Rhod's smile widened to match hers.

"Green . . ."

In the cockpit, the captain and the copilot were going over their post-flight checklist.

The captain looked up and saw the blinking green light.

"Shit!" he said. "Parasites again!"

The copilot looked at the light, pressed a button for a location readout, and shook his head uncomprehendingly.

It wasn't the wheel well.

He got out of his barca and walked to the rear of the cockpit. He reached up and unscrewed an overhead electronics access panel.

The door swung open and Father Cornelius fell out, dangling from a tangle of wires.

"Have we arrived yet?" the priest asked.

# 21

KORBEN HAD ARRIVED.

He knew it as soon as the hostess opened the door of his complimentary stateroom.

He walked in, his eyes glowing. He had never seen such luxury. It was shameless, or shameful, or whatever—but he was not ashamed. What the hell! he thought.

But where was Leeloo?

The bellhop followed him, carrying Leeloo's two bags.

Korben saw a formal invitation on the bedside table.

A complimentary box seat at Diva Plavalaguna's concert, at 5:30. Black tie.

Korben looked at the hostess in confusion.

"For the concert it says formal attire. But I didn't bring anything!"

The hostess ran a fingertip along a touch-sensitive latch, and the closet door slid open.

Korben saw twenty tuxedos, all in his size. In

every color of the rainbow, plus a couple that hadn't yet appeared in nature.

"Welcome to Paradise," said the hostess, closing the closet door.

Korben just stared.

BBBBRRRRRIIIIINNNNNGG!

The hostess put the phone in Korben's hand before he could reach for it.

"Hello?"

"You little sleazebag!"

"Ma?"

Smiling politely, the hostess backed out the door, taking the bellhop with her.

Korben nodded his thanks.

"Don't you ever ask me for another thing in my life again. You've killed your poor mother with your own hands."

Korben found a chair and sat down.

He rolled his eyes at the ceiling, then put the receiver back to his ear.

"Ma . . ."


"All right, Father," said the Fhloston Paradise Security Chief.

He motioned politely and Cornelius sat down in front of the cop's desk.

"Let's hear it."

Cornelius was just about to speak, when the door burst open. A middle-aged cop whose uniform was festooned with communicators, bells, whistles, chains, and security devices of every kind rushed into the Chief's office.

Fog had been a policeman for almost twenty years but he had never lost his initial enthusiasm for the job.

That was the problem, the Chief thought.

"What is it, Fog?" he asked.

"The Diva's ship is coming in, sir!"

"I want maximum secuirity," said the Chief.

"Yes, sir!"

Fog saluted and turned to exit, but the Chief stopped him with a word. "Fog?"

"Yes, sir?"

"Do you know why I told you that?"

"No, sir."

The Chief sighed. Everything had to be explained to Fog.

"Well, listen up. This Diva sings only once every ten years. For three minutes. I have eight thousand people here who have paid a fortune to hear her. Get the picture?"

"Yes, sir," said Fog. He saluted, turned smartly (turning was the only thing he did smartly), and left.

"Okay, Father," the Chief said to Father Cornelius. "Your song now."

"I was in my parish," Cornelius said. "The bell rings, so I open the door and . . ."

The office door banged open again.

Three cops limped in, bloodied and bandaged.

"A bomb?" asked the Chief nervously.

"Yeah," said the only one of the cops who could speak. "A five foot, nine inch bomb with red hair and green eyes."

At this, Cornelius perked up. "Yes!" he said to himself.

A little too loudly.

He looked up to see the three cops and their Chief all staring at him curiously.

Cornelius leaned over the desk toward the Security Chief. "May I speak with you alone?"

*The Diva had arrived!*

Doves flew into the air, and bright jellyfish were released into the water (as stipulated in her contract).

Smoke bombs and flares spattered the sky, and the swelling notes of a brass band announced her arrival to the assembled multitudes (as stipulated in her contract).

She stepped off her tiny private starship onto a red carpet (as stipulated in her contract), and a gang of muscular bodyguards (as stipulated in her contract) cleared her way into the reception deck of the Fhloston Paradise, and down a long corridor.

Those who had come to admire the Diva Plavalaguna's legendary beauty were disappointed, for a white chiffon veil covered her face—though the long tentacles of her "hair" were clearly visible, writhing most appealingly.

Leeloo cut through the crowd of admirers, and headed for the corridor, where she could see the Diva, and be seen by her.

She followed the porters carrying the Diva's voluminous baggage until she was halfway down the corridor, out of sight of the crowd. There she stopped and pretended to admire a painting hanging on the wall.

It was a beautiul rendering of a clipper ship under full sail. It had been knocked askew by the porters and was hanging upside down.

After the porters came the security police, then the bodyguards.

Then the Diva Plavalaguna herself, followed by her managers and personal assistants, numbers one through ten.

Leeloo turned to face the Diva as she passed . . .

And the Diva stopped.

She reached out and touched Leeloo's cheek.

A crackle of static electricity flew between the two women.

The managers and assistants (one through ten) jumped back.

The Diva walked on, followed by her retinue.

Her third associate personal assistant hung back until the rest were gone, then whispered in Leeloo's ear:

"Miss Plavalaguna wants me to tell you that she will give you what you have come to get. But she wants to sing first . . . one last time!"

Leeloo nodded.

"And one other thing . . ."

The assistant turned the painting right side up.

Leeloo smiled. It looked much better.


"Miss Diva . . ."

The Diva approached her dressing room, and found it guarded by a squad of security cops, standing in ranks.

In front of them stood a short, sharp cop hung with medals, devices, insignia, belts, chains, cuffs, whips and a flashlight or two.

"I'm Fog, head of security for your visit."

Diva Plavalaguna ignored him, sweeping past him as if he were a houseplant.

"Everything is in order. You can . . ."

The Diva's retinue followed her, and Fog addressed them as they passed.

". . . make yourselves at home safely. If you need anything . . ."

The dressing room door slammed in his face.

"Give a knock!"


Putting on a tux was difficult enough for Korben, who had quit the military because he hated dressing up (among other reasons).

It was even more difficult with one hand, which was all he had free. With the other he held the phone away from his ear while he tried to placate his mother.

"Listen, Ma! I've only got a few days' vacation, and I don't want to spend them on the phone."

BRRRAAANNNGG!

"Hang on, Ma. It's the door. No! I told you! I didn't bring anybody!"

Korben opened the door of his suite. And saw the most beautiful girl in the galaxy.

"Apipoulai!" Leeloo said with a smile, brushing past him into the suite.

Korben closed the door behind her. "Listen, Ma, I'll call you back . . ."

He hung up the phone.

"You're very cute in your costume," Leeloo said. She found her suitcase on her bed where the bellhop had left it, and pulled out a bright frock.

She laid the dress on the bed and started taking off her clothes.

Korben reddened and turned his back.

"Leeloo, wait a minute! I'm a kind of old-fashioned guy, you know. I'm not saying no—I would love to say yes. But we only met this morning . . ."

"You know," Leeloo said, ignoring his embarrassment, "women normally change clothing five times more than men."

"Oh yeah?" Korben asked. "You get that off the screen?"

"Yes," said Leeloo. "You can turn around."

Korben turned around.

What he saw was only a little more—or less—than what he had both feared and hoped to see.

Leeloo was more beautiful than ever in a short, sharp smock.

"Where are you going?" he asked.

"With you," Leeloo said. "I'm going to see the Diva sing."

Korben was reeling. He had never wanted to feel this way about a woman again. Especially now, when he needed to keep his wits about him. He had to find a way to keep her out of danger.

He sat down heavily on the side of the bed.

Leeloo looked down at her dress—what little there was of it—then back at Korben. "What's the matter? Did I do something wrong?"

"No, not at all," said Korben. "I mean, just the opposite. You're . . . you're *beautiful*!"

Leeloo's face lit up. "Thank you."

Korben shook his head resolutely, then reached into his back pocket. "I have something for you," he said.

Leeloo stood on her tiptoes excitedly. "Gift? For me?"

Korben pulled out a single stainless steel bracelet. "It will go perfectly with your dress."

Leeloo held out her hand. "What do you call it?" she asked, as Korben slipped it over her slim and perfect wrist—and snapped it shut.

"A laser handcuff," he said.

He pressed a button on the side of the cuff, and a laser beam shot from the floor to the ceiling, trapping Leeloo where she stood.

"Army issue, latest model. I'm sorry, Leeloo, but I told you, I have to work in peace."

"You!" she hissed. "You're nothing but a . . ."

"I know exactly the word you're looking for," said Korben. "It's not in the dictionary you studied. I won't be long."

He pulled on his tuxedo jacket.

Just then the door burst open and Loc Rhod rushed in.

"Hey, Stud, we gotta hustle outta here!!"

He saw Leeloo, twisting in her low-cut dress, her hand pinioned above her head by the laser beam.

Loc Rhod smiled.

"Korben, my man, what's happening here?? Who's the chick?? What's the gig?? We free forming here?? Getting funky with this monkey?? Can I get in on this??"Loc Rhod sidled up to the furious Leeloo. He was just reaching for her shapely—

When Korben grabbed him by the collar and lifted him off the floor.

"Later," said Korben, tossing Lod Rhod out the door.

He followed, locking the door carefully behind him.

# 22

A FEW HUNDRED LIGHT YEARS AWAY, THANKS TO THE MAGIC OF FTL technology, President Lindberg and his staff of scientists and generals were listening in on the galaxy's "most happening" radio show.

The President sat at his desk.

The generals were arrayed behind him.

The scientists behind them.

Two speakers emerged from the presidential desktop.

"It's now five P.M. Central Galactic Time, time to join Loc Rhod and Korben Dallas, the lucky winner of the Gemini Croquettes contest . . . Live from Fhloston Paradise!"

Imagine Madison Square Garden, the Grand Canyon, the Eiffel Tower and Albert Hall all wrapped up in one, then hung with gilt and glitter, and filled with low-cut gowns and high-topped shoes.

---

Now triple that, and you have some idea of the magnificence of the Fhloston Paradise Concert Hall.

Korben and Loc Rhod entered side by side.

Korben was scanning the crowd, alert for danger.

Loc Rhod was, as usual, talking, this time into a floating "skeeter-mike" that followed him like a mosquito, hovering near his fast-moving mouth.

"This is probably the most beautiful concert hall in the universe!!" the DJ said. "A perfect replica of an old opera house . . . but who cares!!"

He and Korben passed between rows of gilt seats, all filled with elegantly dressed vacationers and culture-vultures, all (variously) wearing unisex tuxedos, faux-fur robes, jeweled g-strings and voluminous gowns.

"To my left, a row of former ministers, more sinister than minister!! To my right a few generals practicing how to sleep!! And there's Baby Ray, star of stage and screen!!"

With a brief nod of recognition from Loc Rhod, they passed an aging actor whose face was locked in a stiff grin from too many tucks and lifts.

"Ray's drowning in a sea of nymphets!!" said Loc Rhod, "but he's not going to get much out of this concert . . ."

Ray was bending his ear down toward a girl asking for his autograph. "To who?"

". . . since he's stone deaf!! And over there is Roy Von Bacon, the king of laserball and the best-paid player in the league!!"

Loc Rhod reached out to quickly slap hands with an enormous fat man, then sashayed on down the aisle, with Korben following.

"And here we have the Emperor Kodar Japohet, whose daughter Aachen . . ."

Loc Rhod gave the high sign to a white-haired man wearing a rhinestone-trimmed I'M THE EMPEROR, WHO ARE YOU? T-shirt.

". . . is still in my bed!! 'I love to sing,' she recently confessed to me. And now *un peu de champagne* !!"

Loc Rhod grabbed two long-stemmed glasses off a tray held by a handsome, godlike waiter. He handed one to Korben and moved on down the aisle, still babbling into his skeeter-mike.

The waiter handed off the last two glasses of champagne on his tray, then edged through the crowd.

He opened a service door and entered a room filled with "waiters."

Away from the crowd, he relaxed, and his shape-shifting face resolved into the froglike visage of a Mangalore.

Another Mangalore was passing out ZF1 laser rifles.

Akanit, the "waiter" leader, opened the door a crack.

Outside, in the concert hall, the lights were going down.

The first strains of music were coming up.

Akanit smiled a hideous Mangalore smile.
"It's showtime!"

Several decks above the concert hall, in Korben's stateroom, Leeloo was struggling to get free of the laser cuff that held her pinned between ceiling and floor.

Suddenly her sensitive ears picked up a strain of unearthly music.

She tilted her head to one side and smiled in spite of herself.

The music was . . . perfect!

The concert was beginning.

Korben sat beside Loc Rhod in VIP seats on the second row.

The Diva Plavalaguna walked onstage in the dim light.

The lights went down, and a spot showed the Diva herself, unveiled, resplendent in a shimmering blue-green gown.

A human-alien hybrid, the Diva combined in one elegant body the special beauty of all the races in the galaxy (except, of course, the hideous Mangalores).

Her shapely head was topped with a single long, rearward-curving horn. Tentacles descended from her brow like intelligent hair, writhing and waving happily in response to her fans' applause.

Her face, unveiled for the public only once in every decade, was beautiful, soulful, radiant with interstellar emotion.

The music of the three-piece synth-orchestra rose to an introductory crescendo.

The Diva took a deep breath and joined in— and took the music to new heights of emotion and expression.

It was divine, unmatched.

Korben listened, spellbound.

He felt something unfamiliar on his face.

He reached up and touched his cheek, and his fingertips came back wet—

The tears he had always been afraid, as a man, to cry.

Salty tears of joy and sadness, mixed.

Leeloo had stopped struggling to get loose.

She was struggling only to listen.

A song was floating up through the corridors.

The Diva's heavenly voice filled the Fhloston Paradise, vibrating through the hallways and stairwells of the floating hotel until the structure itself was throbbing with unforgettable emotions of love and loss.

Leeloo closed her deep green eyes and let the song wash over her.

Leeloo's tears were sweet, not salty.

On the bridge of Fhloston Paradise, the captain was also listening to the Diva's song—when he was rudely interrupted by a call from the First Officer.

"Captain, I have a ship in trouble. Requesting permission to dock for repairs."

Usually such a request would be denied and the ship sent to the nearest repair facility.

But the music! The deep emotion, the compassion, the unearthly beauty of the Diva's song stirred something in the captain's usually quiet soul.

"Put him in the docking garage," he said.

Then added, as an afterthought: "Inform security."

In the tiny, spartan cockpit of a ZFX200 space fighter orbiting Fhloston, the First Officer's voice came over the speaker.

"Permission granted. Dock 12. You have one hour."

Zorg switched off the com-speaker and leaned back in his barca—and smiled a smile so evil that it would crack the heart of a statue.

"More than I need!"

The Diva's divine music soared through every deck in the immense floating resort hotel.

It filled every heart.

Almost.

One person whose heart was not filled, who was not listening, in fact, was the Diva's manager.

He was in her stateroom, with the door closed to cut down the "noise." He was trying to open a bottle of Scotch that had been sent to the Diva by one of her myriad admirers.

The cap was stuck.

BRRRIIIIINNNG!

It was the doorbell. "Yeah?"

"Flowers for the Diva," came a low, gruff voice.

"She's allergic to flowers," said the manager (who was himself allergic to the Diva).

"There's champagne as well."

"In that case . . ."

The manager set down the recalcitrant Scotch bottle and opened the door.

He found himself staring down the wicked-looking barrel of a ZF1.

A dozen Mangalore warriors dressed in waiters' tuxes pushed past him into the stateroom.

"Hey!" The Diva's manager raised his voice in indignant protest . . .

*Bratabratabrat!*

. . . and took three bullets in the chest.


In the concert hall the music was swelling to higher and higher realms of ecstasy.

Suddenly the Diva opened her eyes and flinched in pain, as if she had been shot . . .

☼     ☼     ☼

In Korben's room, Leeloo suddenly cried out in pain—as if the bullets that had pierced the Diva's manager had pierced her as well.

What was that ruckus?

Father Cornelius was about to leave the Security Chief's office, when he heard footsteps in the corridor outside.

He opened the office door a crack and peered out.

The hallway was filled with Mangalores!

Cornelius watched as a dozen of the hideous creatures, wearing cheap tuxedos and brandishing laser rifles, stormed into the Diva's stateroom three doors down the hall.

"My God!"

He closed the office door.

Leeloo was reeling.

Panicked—as if she had suddenly seen and felt all the horror happening around her.

She looked up toward the ceiling of Korben's stateroom, then down toward the floor—studying the laser beam that held her prisoner.

Her lovely features screwed tight with supreme concentration as she gripped the beam of light in her hands—

And it became solid!

She shattered it, freeing her wrist.

Then, using the beam as a battering ram, she knocked a hole in the ceiling.

She jumped up and grabbed the edge of the hole, then pulled herself through, into the crawl space.

And was gone.

Cornelius ran across the Security Chief's office toward the closet.

He opened the closet door.

There was the Chief, bound and gagged, where the priest had left him.

"Mangalores!" said Cornelius breathlessly. "In the Diva's suite! They want the Sacred Stones! We must stop them!"

"Mmmm!" said the Chief through the duct tape that bound his mouth.

He held up his hands, tied with his own necktie.

Cornelius bent down and started tugging at the knot.

"I'm going to free you, but you must promise to help me!"

The Chief nodded his agreement.

He kept his hands together so that Cornelius wouldn't notice that his fingers were crossed.

"I have it!"

The Mangalore looked up in triumph from the suitcase he was ripping apart. On the floor beside him, the Diva's manager lay in a pool of blood.

The Mangalore warriors had totally trashed the Diva's stateroom, looking for the Sacred Stones.

And now, at last, success!

The lucky Mangalore warrior held up a gold and ivory box, engraved with icons of the four elements—earth, air, fire and water.

He was just about to open it when he heard a commotion above him.

Another Element—this one dedicated to life and peace—was descending from a hole she had ripped in the ceiling panels with one mighty sweep of her delicate hand.

"Apipoulai!" Leeloo said, as she dropped into the stateroom like an avenging angel.

At that precise moment, the Diva Plavalaguna changed both the key and tempo of her song.

Her soaring sonata segued into a funky dance number, picking up the beat and rocking the house.

One of the Managalore warriors whipped out a knife.

A big knife; a giant knife; a monster knife.

He moved on Leeloo.

She disarmed and disabled him with one elegantly graceful (but intensely painful) kick.

The other Mangalores moved in, armed with knives.

Leeloo kicked.

OOOMPH!

Leeloo spun.

AARRGH!

Her kicks and spins became a dance, matching the Diva's rocking beat, and the Managalores fell back, one by one, bloodied and broken.

More Mangalores moved in.

But the music picked up the tempo again, and Leeloo became a whirling dervish, smashing Mangalores against the walls.

In the Concert Hall, the Diva finished her song, and bowed to thunderous applause.

The house was on its feet.

At that exact moment, Leeloo also finished— and bowed ironically to the pitiful groans of the mangled Mangalores lying in heaps around the Diva's demolished stateroom.

The house was on the floor.

But one Mangalore warrior had escaped.

He slipped out the door and ran down the corridor, toward the Concert Hall.

He found Akanit and his warriors standing motionless in the lobby outside the Concert Hall.

Even they had been transfixed by the Diva's music.

"It was an ambush!" the escaped Mangalore whispered into Akanit's drooping, doglike ear.

## The Fifth Element

Akanit heard the story and his already deformed face grew even more monstrous with rage.

"If it's war they want, it's war they'll get!"

He nodded to his hideous warriors.

"Lock and load!"

They cocked their ZF1s.

# 23

CORNELIUS AND THE SECURITY CHIEF ENTERED FHLOSTON Paradise's Central Security Station together.

"You promised!" complained Father Cornelius, who was leading the way—in handcuffs.

The Chief was behind him, holding a gun.

"I had my fingers crossed," said the Chief.


Leeloo picked up the gold and ivory box from the floor where the Mangalore had dropped it.

Her eyes brightened when she saw the engraved icons of the four elements.

She was just about to open it—

When the door to the stateroom burst open!

Zorg stood in the doorway, holding a ZF1.

"My compliments, little lady!" he said, his eyes quickly scanning the chaotic scene. "Thanks for doing all the dirty work. I couldn't have done it better myself!"

His voice grew cold and the ZF1 hummed nastily.

"Now hand over the stones."

Leeloo smiled and tossed the box to Zorg.

Zorg fumbled, barely catching it—

And when he looked back, he saw Leeloo leaping high into the air. With one Olympic-class flip, she disappeared into the hole from which she had descended.

Furious, Zorg sprayed the ceiling with fire.

*Bratbratbrat!*

The crawl space was dark, but the bullets raining through opened little points of light, like stars.

*Bratbratbrat!Bratbratbrat!*

Leeloo danced from side to side, avoiding the bullets as she ran.

*Bratbratbrat!Bratbratbrat!Bratbratbrat!*

Zorg emptied his clip.

*Bratbratbrat!Bratbratbrat!Bratbratbrat!*

The door to the Central Security Station exploded inward, riddled with bullets.

A dozen Mangalores rushed in, firing their ZF1s.

"Nobody move!" growled Akanit. "We're taking over this ship!"

The Security Chief hit the floor, Cornelius beside him.

"I hate to say 'I told you,'" said Cornelius. "But I told you!"

Fog had stationed himself at the rear of the Concert Hall, where he could watch everything and still hear the Diva Plavalaguna's magnificent song.

And a magnificent song it was.

She was taking her tenth curtain call and he was applauding wildly with the rest of the crowd, when—

WHAP!

The door from the lobby flew open, knocking him off his feet and rattling all his dangling devices.

Three Mangalores rushed into the Concert Hall.

"Everybody down!" they shouted.

Then they started shooting.

*Bratbratbrat!Bratbratbrat!Bratbratbrat!*

The general alarm went off:

RAREARAREARAREA!

Zorg tossed away his empty clip. He was just about to reload his ZF1, when he heard a distant alarm:

RAREARAREARAREA!

The general alarm!

"I know this music," he said, chuckling to himself.

He loved chaos and confusion; and he knew just how to add to it!

Reaching into his pocket, he pulled out a small cylindrical device.

A mini-nuke.

"Let's change the beat!" he said.

He stuck the bomb to the wall and flicked a tiny switch.

The timer started counting down.

30:00

29:59

With a sick, triumphant smile, Zorg put the gold and ivory box under his arm and ran out of the stateroom.

"Ladies and gentlemen!!" Loc Rhod shouted into his hovering skeeter-mike. "Something's happening here!! I think we are being attacked!!"

"No shit," Korben muttered softly.

*Bratbratbrat!Bratbratbrat!Bratbratbrat!*

"The Concert Hall is crawling with armed aliens!" cried the excited DJ.

*BuddhabuddhaBuddhabuddhaBuddhabuddha!*

Fog's security guards were firing back.

Fog himself staggered to his feet, cuffs and chains clanking, and reached for his gun.

It was not in his holster!

He spotted it on the floor where it had fallen, and dove for it.

He pulled the trigger.

*clikclikclik—*

Jammed!

Fog stood up, trying to unjam his gun, when the Mangalores spotted his badge (or badges) and fired.

*Bratbratbrat!Bratbratbrat!Bratbratbrat!*

The fusillade sent him diving through an access door into a small storage room.

*Bratbratbrat!Bratbratbrat!*
*BuddhabuddhaBuddhabuddha*

Korben scanned the Concert Hall, trying to figure out which force was firing at whom.

Then it became a moot point.

The Diva was hit.

*Bratabrat!*

Once, twice!

She spun around, doubled over—

And fell off the stage, straight into Korben's arms!

Korben lowered her to the floor, out of the line of fire.

Ignoring the panic all around, he wrapped her in his dinner jacket, trying desperately to stop, or at least slow, the flow of bright blue blood.


The door of the docking garage opened.

A ZFX200 rocketed out, speeding away from Fhloston Paradise, into the high, white fluffy clouds.

Zorg sat at the controls, his scarred face twisted into a happy rictus of demonic joy.

He patted the gold and ivory box on the seat beside him.

"If you want something done," he said to himself smugly, "do it yourself!"

Korben set the Diva's head on the floor as gently as possible. Her eyes were fluttering . . .

Loc Rhod was crouched behind his seat nearby, rapping non-stop into his still-hovering skeeter-mike:

"They're hideous!! They've got a crest on their heads, the eyes of a toad, and fingers all over their hands. Totally hideous!!"

Half a galaxy away, in the President's office, the assembled scientists and generals were listening intently to the radio broadcast.

"Totally hideous!!" rapped Loc Rhod.

"Mangalores!" said General Munro.

President Lindberg had already figured it out. "Send a battalion immediately!"

"I was sent by the government to help you," Korben said to the Diva Plavalaguna. "I guess I blew it!"

"Don't worry," the alien beauty whispered. "This is my fate." Her eyes fluttered. "How was the concert?"

Korben was shocked. She was dying and all she cared about was how she had sounded?

But why not? She was, after all, an artist.

"I've never heard anything so beautiful!" he said—quite truthfully.

The Diva smiled weakly. Already her voice sounded as if it were coming from far away.

"You're a good man," she whispered. "She was right to choose you . . ."

Korben thought he had misheard. "Who?"

"The Fifth Element. The Supreme Being. Sent to Earth to save the Universe."

Korben was stunned. "Do you mean . . . ?"

The Diva nodded. "Leeloo. You must give her the Sacred Stones. She's the only one who knows how to use them!"

*Bratbratbrat!Bratbratbrat!Bratbratbrat!*
*BuddhabuddhaBuddhabuddha!*

Korben looked up. The battle was still raging. He pulled out his gun.

"But she needs your help," the Diva went on. "And your love. She's more fragile than she seems."

Korben crouched and blasted two attacking Mangalores.

They fell back into the cheap seats, screaming in pain.

"Yeah, so am I!" said Korben.

The Diva took his hand and pulled him back down beside her.

"She was created to protect life, not to live it. If you want her to live, she must learn how to love!"

Her eyes closed.

☼    ☼    ☼

The door to the Diva's stateroom swung open noiselessly.

The housekeeping robot looked in, beeped twice, and trundled on.

On the wall, the little cylinder glowed and the liquid crystal counter turned over.

20:00

19:59

"You can't die!" Korben said.

He slapped the Diva's cheeks gently.

Her eyes were closed. Her gown was soaked blue with blood.

"We have the world to save here, remember? You hear me? Where are the Sacred Stones?"

Her eyelids fluttered. Just barely.

It could have been from Korben's breath.

*Orbit Achieved* said the readout on the instrument panel of the ZFX200.

Zorg floated up from his seat. The little ship was so primitive—no faux grav!

But what did Zorg care? He had what he had come for! He grabbed the gold and ivory box that was floating nearby.

It was *deja vu* all over again.

Empty!

"Where are the stones!?!"

The Diva's eyes opened one last time.

On Korben Dallas, cab driver, one-time war hero, now intent on saving the Universe.

She smiled weakly.

One last smile.

"The stones . . . are with me. . . ."

And the blue blood flowed from her mouth, and she closed her eyes for the last time, and she died in Korben's arms.


In the crawl space above the Diva's stateroom, Leeloo clutched herself, in sudden indescribable pain.

"NNNNOOOooooooo!"

# 24

"HANDS ON YOUR HEAD!"

Korben looked around and saw that the Mangalores now controlled the aisles, the stage, the entrances and the exits to the Concert Hall.

They were in total control.

"Everyone!" said a Mangalore.

"My man!!" Loc Rhod hissed. He was hidden a few feet away from Korben, under a row of seats. "I think we should, like, listen to them!!"

"Give me a minute," said Korben. He was studying the still form of the Diva, repeating her last words:

"*The stones are with me. With me?*"

"Hey! You!"

Korben's reverie was broken by the rude knobby hand of a Mangalore, who grabbed him by the collar and pulled—

—only to be yanked off his feet by a lightning judo move and flipped over Korben's shoulder to land flat on his lizard-skin ass with a—

WHUMP!

When the Mangalore opened his eyes he saw Korben crouched over him. Korben's gun was in the alien warrior's mouth.

"I *said* give me a *minute*!"

Korben motioned to Loc Rhod, who crept out of hiding.

"Hold this," said Korben. He put the handle of his gun in Loc Rhod's hand, leaving the barrel stuck in the open mouth of the petrified Mangalore.

"Oh, man, Korben . . ." complained Loc Rhod.

But Korben wasn't listening.

He was kneeling over the body of the Diva Plavalaguna, repeating her dying words to himself as if they were a mantra:

"*The stones are with me—the stones are with me—*"

Korben pressed down on the Diva's stomach.

It was soft.

Then hard.

"*The stones are in me?*"

Hesitating for only an instant, he plunged his hand into the gaping wound in the Diva's side.

And pulled out a Sacred Stone.

"Yes!"

Startled by Korben's shout, Loc Rhod flinched.

*BLAM!*

The top flew off of the Mangalore's head. His brains spattered the apron of the stage.

"Oh, man!!" said Loc Rhod. "I'm sorry!"

✿    ✿    ✿

Korben pulled out another stone, then another, then another.

All four were covered with bright blue blood.

He tore off his shirt and wrapped the stones in it, then handed the bundle to Loc Rhod.

"Lose these stones and I promise, you'll look like him."

Korben pointed to the dead Mangalore. "Got it?"

"Green!" said Loc Rhod. "Super green!"

"Good. Follow me!"


"Green. Super Green!"

Loc Rhod's words came loud and clear through the twin speakers on the desk of the President of the United Federation.

The President wiped his face with a towel. "How many people do you think are listening to this?" he asked one of his scientists.

"Around fifty-two billion, sir."

The President turned to General Munro. "Is that your idea of a discreet operation?"

"Don't worry, sir," Munro said nervously (though he looked worried himself). "I know my man Dallas. He'll calm things down."

"He damn well better!"

✿    ✿    ✿

CRASH!

The glass doors of the Concert Hall burst into a thousand pieces as two Mangalore warriors were thrown through them, into the hall.

Behind them came Korben, a ZF1 in each hand.

"Everybody down!" he yelled, as he swept the lobby with laser fire, mowing down the retreating Mangalores.

*BratbratbratBratbratbrat!*
*BratbratbratBratbratbrat!*

Answering fire echoed from the right, and Korben hit the deck, rolling behind a massive fluted column.

Loc Rhod slid in beside him, still rapping to his hovering skeeter-mike.

"This is amazing!! Korben, Korben Dallas, winner of the Gemini Croquettes contest, just killed three warriors like he was swatting flies!!"

*Bratbratbrat!*

Two more Mangalores were firing at the column, shredding it into shards of sharp shrapnel.

*Barang! Kahwang!*

"Come on!" said Korben, and he half dove, half rolled across the lobby to the intermission bar.

"No way!!" said Loc Rhod. While the Mangalores were concentrating on Korben, the agile DJ scurried up a curtain to the balcony, where he continued commenting on the action below.

BARRAP BARRAP BARRAP!

Another Mangalore was using his ZF1 as a missile launcher, destroying the intermission bar piece by piece. The missiles were getting closer and closer to Korben.

*clikityclik!*

Korben's ZF1 was empty. Looking desperately around the lobby, he saw an abandoned laser rifle on a nearby pool table.

The galactic film star Baby Ray was hiding under the pool table.

"Toss me the gun!" Korben shouted.

"What?" Baby Ray poked his head out, just as another missile chewed up another section of the bar.

"The gun, for Christ's sake!" Korben shouted. He pointed at the ZF1, which lay amid a cluster of pool balls.

"Oh," said Baby Ray.

He rolled the pool balls across the floor toward Korben.

"Thanks," said Korben sarcastically. "That'll sure help!"

"Hands up!"

Korben looked up.

A Mangalore was looking over the bar, a ZF1 in hand.

"Stand up. Slow!"

Korben stood up.

Slow.

Still moving slowly and deliberately, he climbed atop the bar. The Mangalore was standing on a fallen ceiling panel balanced on a bullet-riddled Mangalore corpse.

"Down!" said the Mangalore.

"Okay," said Korben obligingly.

He stepped off the bar, onto the panel.

It seesawed, sending the Mangalore on the other end flying straight up.

The Mangalore's hideous head rammed through the balcony and stopped—an inch from Loc Rhod's terrified face.

"Yeeeeaaaahhh!!"

"Yech!" responded the Mangalore, face to face with the DJ.

The alien's battle-honed reflex depressed the trigger finger on his gun, which sprayed the lobby with laser bullets—

*Bratbratbrat!*

—three of which took out three other Mangalores running toward Korben.

WHAK!

Loc Rhod stopped the firing by hitting the Mangalore on the head with the shirtful of stones.

"Sorry, man!!"

*Bratbratbrat!*

Three more Mangalores burst into the balcony, guns blazing.

"Korben, man!!" cried Loc Rhod. "Help!!"

"Don't move!" said Korben.

Rolling over until he was under the balcony, he fired his entire clip straight up, chewing a circle out of the balcony—which dropped Lod Rhod onto the floor at Korben's feet.

"Oooof!!" said the DJ, at a loss for words, for once.

Loc Rhod watched curiously as Korben broke his empty gun in half, removing an inner magazine which he threw overhand at the underside of the balcony.

It stuck, and a light started flashing.

"What're you doing?" the DJ asked.

"You'll know in a ten seconds! Nine, eight . . . Come on!"

Korben grabbed Loc Rhod and pulled him toward the pool table. Seeing that the table was on casters, the DJ knew just what to do. Together, the two men pushed the pool table into the long sloping aisle of the Concert Hall, and climbed under it as soon as it started rolling.

*Bratbratbrat!*

The Mangalores on the balcony fired down. The green felt tabletop exploded into fragments, but no bullets penetrated to the bottom, where Korben and Loc Rhod were hiding.

The table rolled faster and faster. . . .

*BAAARRRROOM!*

The balcony disappeared in a wall of flame.

The Concert Hall was suddenly very quiet.

Very quiet.

Korben and Loc Rhod emerged from underneath the pool table. Korben picked up a ZF1 that had fallen to the floor.

Suddenly a service door opened at the side of the hall.

Korben spun, gun at the ready.

A middle-aged cop stepped out. He was festooned with badges and devices, and he held his gun at the ready.

"Nobody move!"

"Huh??" Loc Rhod looked from the funny little cop to Korben.

"I am Captain Fog, in charge of concert security."

"Good," said Korben. "You're just the man I was looking for."

He tossed the little man the big ZF1.

"You're in charge."

Then he grabbed Loc Rhod by the arm and marched him out of the hall.

# 25

"LEELOO?"

Korben's cry was half hope, half desperation, as he burst into the stateroom of the dear departed Diva.

The room was a shambles, tossed by the Mangalores, then shot up by Zorg.

But Korben hardly noticed the blood, the bodies, the belongings scattered around the floor.

He saw only the luminous bar of laser chain, shattered and scattered on the floor, flickering dimly as it gradually faded out of existence. He saw only the hole in the ceiling through which Leeloo had made her escape.

"Leeloo!!??"

He was so desperate to find her, that he ran back out of the stateroom as soon as he saw she was gone.

He didn't hear the faint answer to his cry that came from the crawl space above the ceiling.

Leeloo was weak. She was bleeding and battered, but she had heard him.

"Kor . . . ben . . ."

He didn't see the mini-nuke stuck to the wall, or the liquid crystal display still counting down:

10:00

9:59

Meanwhile, in nearby outer space, a ZFX 200 had just made a U-turn and was heading back toward Fhloston Paradise.

Zorg was at the controls, as blind to the beauties of intragalactic interstellar space as he was to the virtues of kindness and compassion.

An empty box lay torn to pieces on the cockpit floor.

Zorg was muttering darkly:

"I am not happy. At all."

Meanwhile, at Fhloston Paradise Central Security Headquarters, the last remnants of the Mangalore raiding party had barricaded themselves in the back of the station.

They were under siege by the cops, but they still had plenty of ammunition, and they were shooting at anything that moved, much less tried to enter.

Korben arrived, still searching for Leeloo. He found Fog among the cops in the corridor.

"You still in charge?"

"Yes, sir," answered Fog.

"How many in there?"

"I don't know."

"Let's count," suggested Korben.

He went to the door and stuck his head around. Cautiously, so as not to excite the warriors inside.

"Seven to the left," he said. "Five to the right."

Fog nodded obediently but uncomprehendingly. So what?

Korben stuck his head around again—this time accompanied by his ZF1.

*Bratbratbrat!Bratbratbrat!Bratbratbrat!*

"Six to the left, one to the right," muttered Korben, reloading. "We got to find the leader."

"Leader?" Fog echoed.

"Mangalores don't fight without a leader."

As if in answer to Korben's observation, a stir came from inside the station.

Akanit stood up.

He dragged Father Cornelius out into the open, where he could be seen.

He held a gun to the back of the old priest's head.

"One more shot and we start killing hostages," Akanit said. "Got that?"

"Found the leader," muttered Korben.

"Send someone in to negotiate," shouted Akanit.

"Mind if I go?" Korben asked Fog. "I'm an excellent negotiator."

Fog nodded. His medals clinked.

He stood up and shouted back: "We're sending someone in who's authorized to negotiate!"

Korben stood and walked quickly through the door. He walked straight up to Akanit and put a bullet through his head.

As the Mangalore leader toppled and fell, Korben turned to the other confused and milling warriors:

"Anyone else want to negotiate?"


Fog was impressed. "Where'd he learn to negotiate like that?" he mused aloud.

The President, who had been monitoring the entire operation from his office, looked hard at General Munro.

"I wonder," he also mused aloud.

Munro squirmed under the President's glare and looked away.

# 26

WHILE THE POLICE ROUNDED UP THE REMAINING, STUNNED Mangalores, Korben went to the Central Security control panel and searched the bank of view screens that showed every corner of Fhloston Paradise.

Looking . . . looking . . . looking . . .

"You're probably very angry with me," said a voice at his side.

Korben turned and saw Father Cornelius.

"I understand," the priest went on. "But I want you to know I'm fighting for a noble cause."

"Yeah, I know, to save the world," said Korben, still searching. "But all I want to do is find Leeloo."

Cornelius was alarmed. "Leeloo's in trouble?"

"When is she *not* in trouble?" muttered Korben.

"Hi, guys!!" said Loc Rhod, who was back. Skeeter-mike, bundle, and all.


*Brrriinng!*
Incoming.

The docking garage officer opened the door.

A ZFX200 settled into the dock.

It looked familiar.

"More trouble?" the officer asked the pilot.

"Nothing I can't handle myself," said Zorg. He raised his ZF1—

*Bratbratbrat! Bratbratbrat!*


Korben knew pursuit.

It was a science.

First Principle: Always return to the last place you saw your quarry.

He went back to the Diva's ruined stateroom.

Loc Rhod and Cornelius tagged along.

The housekeeping and coroner 'bots had cleared out the bodies, but the room was still a wreck, with a huge hole in the ceiling.

"Leeloo!" Korben yelled.

While Korben checked out the closets, the bath, the kitchenette, Loc Rhod studied the malevolent looking device stuck to the wall.

"Korben, man . . ." he asked. "What is this??"

Korben glanced at it. "A molecular bomb. A mini-nuke."

"What are these numbers clicking by??" Loc Rhod asked.

3:01

3:00

2:59

"Probably the time remaining before it

explodes," said Father Cornelius, as he helped Korben with the search for Leeloo.

Loc Rhod smiled; or tried to smile. "You guys are just saying that to scare me, right? There are bomb detectors in all these hotels. If this was a bomb, the alarm would have gone off."

At that exact moment, a siren sounded, followed by a loud robotic voice:

"THIS.IS.A.TYPE.A.ALERT! FOR.SECURITY. REASONS.THE.HOTEL.MUST.BE.EVACU-ATED."

Father Cornelius and Korben continued their search.

Loc Rhod looked stunned.


In the hallways of the great ship, the reaction was more dramatic.

"TYPE.A.ALERT!PLEASE.PROCEED.CALMLY. TO.THE.LIFEBOATS.LOCATED.IN.THE.MAIN. HALLWAYS."

Crowds stampeded toward the exits, trampling the fallen underfoot. Screams ripped through the air and shots rang out as the panicking masses surged through the corridors, looking for the lifeboats.

Panic!

Just as it seemed the situation could get no worse, Zorg emerged from the docking garage, cradling his ZF1 at waist level and blasting everything and everyone in sight.

*Bratbratbratbrat!Bratbratbratbrat!Bratbratbrat brat!*

Fog flattened himself against the wall and blew a whistle, then shouted as authoritatively as possible: "Please stay calm! We have the situation totally under control . . ."

His words were lost in the general melee.


1:59
   1:58
Loc Rhod stood paralyzed as the display on the molecular mini-nuke counted down. He watched with the helpless fascination of a mouse watching the uncoiling cobra that is about to devour him.

"Like, D-Man!!" he said, "I hate to bother you . . ."

Korben came out of the bedroom, which he had just finished searching.

". . . but we're down to, like, two minutes here!!"

Korben joined the DJ at the bomb.
   1:43
   1:42

"It's the latest model," Korben said, studying it. "I've never seen one before. Let's see if I can disable it. I need a pin . . ."

Without taking his eyes off the bomb, he pulled a hairpin from Loc Rhod's elaborate "do."

☼     ☼     ☼

Only four feet above, Leeloo was looking down from the crawl space, through one of the holes Zorg had blasted in the ceiling.

She was too weak to make a sound, bleeding badly from a wound in her side that exactly matched the Diva's.

She stuck her finger in the blood, then stuck her bloody finger through one of the holes in the ceiling.

It was right above Korben, who was trying to disarm the bomb with the hairpin.

The drop of blood spattered on his hand.

Korben looked up.

"Hey, what are you doing??" Loc Rhod demanded. "The bomb!!"

Ignoring him, Korben dragged a desk directly under the hole. He jumped up on it, and stuck his head into the crawl space.

Leeloo rewarded him with a weak but tender smile.

"Don't worry," Korben said. "I'm here now!"

He pulled her down from the shaft and laid her gently on the desk.

"Just relax," he said, "We've got the Sacred Stones. Everything's going to be fine."

Loc Rhod wasn't so sure.

The timer read

00:32

00:31

"Korben," he said, "can I have, like, thirty seconds of your time here??"

Korben ran his fingertips along Leeloo's cheek. "I'll be right back!"

He turned back to the bomb, and began probing it with the hairpin. Loc Rhod stood as still as a statue, studying the liquid crystal display:

00:22
00:21

Even the skeeter-mike at Loc Rhod's mouth was motionless.

Korben felt something tickle the back of his neck. He turned and found himself staring into the barrel of a ZF1.

At the other end of the formidable laser rifle— was Zorg!

The demented billionaire smuggler pulled a plastic credit card with a magnetic strip from his shirt pocket.

"Do you mind?" he asked with a smile.

Loc Rhod and Korben both stared.

00:14
00:13

Zorg swiped the card through a slot on the side of the bomb.

*Bleeeeeep!* The timer reset.

05:00
04:59

"Overtime!" said Zorg.

Loc Rhod fainted. The faithful skeeter-mike followed him to the floor.

☼    ☼    ☼

Zorg ignored the unconscious DJ. He kept the gun trained on Korben.

"Well, what do we have here? Is this Korben Dallas? The famous winner of the Gemini Croquettes contest? Or is this Korben Dallas from Special Section sent by General Munro and President Lindberg himself?"

Korben looked concerned.

"You know, Mr. Zorg," he said, "this kind of weapon is very dangerous. You can hurt somebody with this puppy."

"Yes?" Zorg smiled. "Isn't that the purpose of it?"

"Good thing it's not loaded," said Korben.

"Oh really?" said Zorg, who had heard this old trick several times before.

"Really," said Korben. "You see that yellow flashing light on the side? It tells you the safety is on."

"Nice try," said Zorg (although he didn't really mean it). "But you see, I built this weapon myself, and I know exactly how it works. The yellow light doesn't mean the safety is on. It means the clip is . . ."

Ooops.

". . . empty."

"Good to know," said Korben. He drew back his ham-sized fist.

Slowly.

Savoring the anticipation.

Zorg tried to fire:
*clickityclickityclick.*

"A three-thousand round clip!" Zorg said. "Surely I didn't fire three-thousand rounds!"

"You should learn to count," said Korben. "It's not all that hard. Watch, and I'll show you."

*CRUNCH!* He punched Zorg in the face.

"One. That's for firing me."

*CRUNCH!*

"Two. That's for trying to kill me. And . . ."

*CRUNCH! CRUNCH! CRUNCH!*

"And the rest is for what you did to my wife!"

*Wife?* Zorg wondered, just before his lights went out.


Several hundred light years away, the President and his general reacted very differently to the brutal sounds coming over the sound link from Loc Rhod's open mike.

President Lindberg closed his eyes, whether in pain or delight it was hard to tell.

General Munro moved his shoulders like a boxer, as if it were he, rather than Korben, pummeling Zorg.


03:00
    02:59
    "We're running out of time again!" said Father Cornelius.

"We're outta here," said Korben. He picked up Leeloo in his massive arms and headed for the door.

Loc Rhod was still passed out on the floor. Father Cornelius knelt beside him and awakened him with a slap.

Loc Rhod sat up.

"Are you nuts, Father?? That, like, hurt!! I can't feel my teeth!!"

"It doesn't matter," said Cornelius, pulling the DJ to his feet. He shoved the bloody shirt containing the Sacred Stones into his arms. "All you need are your legs!"

# 27

"DON'T PUSH," SAID FOG. "THERE'S PLENTY OF ROOM!"

Nobody was fooled.

The enormous crowd filled the corridor, pushing toward the tiny lifeboats.

Loc Rhod's three assistants found themselves near the front.

"Hurry up ladies . . . er, gentlemen," said Fog, who had been fooled at first by their unisex outfits.

The three stopped, looking around for their boss, their mentor, their hero, icon, and legendary leader, Loc Rhod.

"We can't go without our master!" said the first.

"We WON'T go without our master," said the second.

"Absolutely NOT!" said the third.

"This is the last boat," said Fog.

Three identical faces fell.

"Maybe he already left," said the first.

"I think I saw him leave," said the second.

"I KNOW I saw him go!" said the third.

And all three piled into the boat as it cut loose from the hovering luxury hotel.

"TWO.MINUTES.TO.COMPLETE.EVACUA-TION!" said the loudspeaker, as Korben, Leeloo, Loc Rhod and Father Cornelius raced to the docking garage.

Korben broke the lock on the first ship he saw that looked spaceworthy—

Zorg's ZFX200.

In the dead Diva's savaged suite, Zorg was coming around.

He raised his bruised and battered head and looked for his gun.

The liquid crystal counter read:

01:12

01:11

In the ZFX200, Korben swept the broken box off the copilot's seat, and set Leeloo down.

He gently strapped her in.

Loc Rhod and Cornelius crowded into the tiny cockpit behind them.

Zorg picked up his ZF1 and studied it.

"I didn't fire three thousand rounds. Did I?"


"ONE.MINUTE.TO.TOTAL.EVACUATION," droned the loudspeaker.

"You know how to fly this thing??" Loc Rhod asked.

Korben strapped himself into the pilot's barca. "It's like a cab, isn't it?" he asked drily.

Loc Rhod winced.

"THIRTY.SECONDS.UNTIL . . ."

"Anyone know how to open the garage door?" Korben asked.

Loc Rhod shook his head.

Cornelius shook his head.


Zorg was still studying his empty gun when the display on the bomb flashed.

*Bleep!*

Ten second warning!

00:09

00:08

Zorg pushed a hidden button on the side of the ZF1 and held it directly over his head.

A mauve-colored magnetic force field descended from the gun, enveloping him in an indestructible protective sarcophagus.

✿　　✿　　✿

"EIGHT.SEVEN . . ."

The robotic loudspeaker had patched into the mini-nuke's countdown.

Loc Rhod and Korben searched frantically through the switches and dials on the dashboard of the ZFX200.

"Found it?" Korben asked.

Loc Rhod shook his head. "I don't even know what I'm looking for!"

Father Cornelius pointed to a row of buttons. "Press them all," he said.

"Good idea," said Korben, fingertips already flying.

Servos whined.

Magnetic motors howled into service.

Valves opened and solenoids clicked.

A battery of guns emerged from the front of the tiny fighter—all pointed toward the garage door.

An auto gun trigger emerged from the dash.

"Found it," said Korben.

"BLAMBLAMBLAM!!

A storm of cannonfire erupted from the nose of the ZFX200, blasting the garage door off its hinges.

"Hold on tight!"

Korben pushed the throttle forward.

The little ship rocketed out of the side of the great luxury liner, into the azure sky over the turquoise sea.

✿ ✿ ✿

00:02
  00:01
  00:*BHAAARRRROOOOOOOOOOOOM!*
The Diva's suite disappeared.
The corridor disappeared.
The dirty laundry disappeared.
The Concert Hall and intermission bar disappeared.
All in a hellish, scorching wave of destruction.
The passengers, safe in their tiny lifeboats, watched in horror as the magnificent luxury liner itself disappeared, consumed in a ball of flame—
From which only a tiny spacefaring jet, the ZFX200, emerged, coasting on up into the clouds, just ahead of the gigantic shock wave.


Cornelius breathed out, realizing as he did that he had been holding his breath for several minutes.
"Just like a cab," quipped Korben, leaning back in his pilot's barca.
Loc Rhod checked his watch, then made sure his skeeter-mike was still open—and had picked up the sounds of the blast and the escape.
He rapped:
"Dear listeners, your favorite DJ is alive and kicking!! It's seven o'clock, Galactic Standard Time, and time for the news!! Tune in tomorrow for another adventure with yours truly—

"Loc Rhod!!"

He hit a tiny switch.

*Bleep!*

End of transmission.

Loc Rhod leaned back and let out a huge, satisfied sigh. He looked up to see Father Cornelius and Korben both watching him.

He grinned weakly. "Best show I ever did!"

General Munro entered the President's office.

He was smiling: an unusual configuration temporarily softening the rough military terrain that was his face.

"Major Dallas has the Five Elements on board," Munro said. "The Priest is guiding them directly to the Temple."

President Lindberg closed his eyes in relief.

"Thank God. We're saved!"

The blast wave from the explosion of the Fhloston Paradise carried out in waves like the ripples from a stone thrown into a pond.

Big stone. Big pond. Big ripples.

Flying at the leading edge of the cloud of dust, debris and detritus was a mauve magnetic digital sarcophagus, which tumbled end over end over end, and . . .

Fell into a snowbank on an untracked glacier, high on the shoulder of an inaccessible range of

unexplored peaks near the middle of an unmapped
polar continent.

THWUNK!


High in the towers of Manhattan, in Zorg's office,
the phone was ringing.

The secretary paused in her task of polishing
her nails, long enough to pick it up.

"Yes?"

"ZXXDXDX those damned XXSSZXC!"

"Oh, Mr. Zorg. I was so worried."

"I was ZXZXZXSW in the ZXZXS!"

"Sorry, I can't hear you so well."


High in the polar mountains of the planet
Fhloston, a figure clambered out of a sarcophagus-
shaped hole in the snow.

Zorg.

Bruised, battered, bloodied . . . but unbowed.

He was carrying a cellular phone.

"Can you hear me better now?"

"Yes, Mr. Zorg, I can hear you perfectly. How
was the concert?"

"Listen up, instead of running off at the mouth!
My batteries are almost gone."

"Sorry, sir!"

"Send me another ZFX200, immediately!"

"Right away, sir. I'll send it to the hotel."

"I'm not *at* the hotel! There *is* no hotel!"

*Bleeep.*

"Hello! Hello!"

*Battery dead.*

Silence.

A silence broken only by the cold howling of the polar wind.

Zorg sat down on a hummock of ice. "I need to think," he muttered.


President Lindberg and his military staff were toasting their success with champagne, when suddenly a worried looking scientist burst into the office.

All scientists look worried.

This one looked more worried than usual.

"Mr. President—"

"Yes?" Lindberg said impatiently. "Now what?"

"There's a small problem."

The scientist nodded toward a tech, who touched a panel on the office window, turning it into a long-distance galactic viewscreen.

The display, patched in from a pursuing warship, showed a planet-sized ball of dark fire hurtling across the nether regions of space.

"It's moving?" asked the President.

"It's not only moving," cut in the commander of the pursuing warship. "It's moving at incredible speed. We're having trouble following it."

The President turned to the scientist who had brought him the bad news.

"Any idea where it's heading?"
The scientist gulped.
Then nodded.
"Here."

# 28

THERE IS NOWHERE MORE PEACEFUL THAN SPACE.

The little ZFX200 rocked gently as it sped through the interlaced layers of Space Time, pulled at a high multiple of the speed of light by the tightly twisted strands of the superstring plasma drive.

Korben was paying no attention. He had put the ship on autopilot.

All his attention was focused on the lovely being that lay resting in his arms.

He wiped Leeloo's perfect forehead.

She opened her green eyes.

"Apipoulai," whispered Korben.

Leeloo rewarded him with a smile that outdazzled the myriad stars flashing past.

"The Diva asked me to look after you," Korben said.

"Humans act . . . so strange . . ." she whispered weakly.

"What do you mean?"

"Everything you create . . . is used to destroy . . ."

"We call that human nature," said Korben. "Didn't you learn that off the screen, scrolling through the database?"

"Not finished yet . . ." said Leeloo. "I'm only up to V."

"You still have some good words coming."

"Like what . . . ?"

"Like valiant. Like vulnerable. Like very, very . . ."

"Excuse me!"

Their moment of romantic reverie was broken by a loud *BBBRRRRIIIINNNNG!*

Father Cornelius answered the phone in the rear of the cockpit.

"It's a General Mambo."

"Munro," corrected Korben. He turned on the computer in front of Leeloo and kissed the universe's loveliest forehead.

"Finish your lesson. I'll be right back."

Leeloo watched glowingly as Korben got out of his barca to answer the phone.

She turned back to the computer screen. She scrolled past V, to W.

WAR. The word was illustrated with pictures from humankind's history.

The Civil War, World War II, the Trojan War, the Vietnam War . . .

Tears began flowing in parallel streams down the universe's two loveliest cheeks.

☼ ☼ ☼

The first thing Korben heard when he picked up the phone was a throat clearing.

Not a military but a presidential throat.

"Major Dallas, I would first like to salute a warrior, a true combatant, a shining example of this Army's might. In the name of the Federation and its territories, and all who fight for freedom and democracy . . ."

Korben shook the receiver impatiently.

"Mr. President, why don't you just get to the point? What's the problem?"

The President let out a deep sigh. "There's a ball of fire twelve hundred miles in diameter heading straight for Earth. And we have no idea how to stop it. That's the problem."

"How much time before impact?"

There was a moment's delay while the President consulted with his scientific staff. "If its speed remains constant—one hour and fifty-seven minutes."

"I'll call you back in two hours," said Korben. He hung up.

The President fell back into his chair, filled with despair.

Korben climbed back into the pilot's barca of the little ZFX200 . . .

And kicked in the ultra-turbos!

☼ ☼ ☼

Less than an hour later, the spacecraft was parked on the sand, under a desert sun.

Korben got out, carrying the unconscious Leeloo in his arms. Loc Rhod followed, still carrying the Sacred Stones wrapped in the blue-bloodied shirt.

Father Cornelius was already busy, digging with his hands into the side of a dune.

Korben interrupted him. "Father," he said. "Your temple. Where is the entrance?"

"It's here somewhere," said the old priest. "But one year the dune is on the left of the entrance, and the next year it's on the right . . ."

He resumed digging.

Loc Rhod was already staggering in the heat.

"I can't take it any more!!" he said. "I'm a celebrity!! I'm not cut out to be a hero in real life, just to play one on the radio!! Just bury me where I fall!!"

And he dropped, exhausted, onto the sand.

Which moved under him.

"Yikes!!"

Loc Rhod jumped up just as a trap door opened in the sand underneath him.

The young novice, David, emerged. "Thank God you're here!"

Korben called to Cornelius, who was still digging in the loose sand:

"Found it!"

❀     ❀     ❀

President Lindberg was dozing fitfully in his chair.

An aide entered the office and woke him gently.

"They've just landed in the desert."

The President wiped the presidential forehead, a regular Rushmore of a brow. "How much time left?"

The aide pointed to the viewscreen on the wall.

It showed a small, blue planet, glowing like a precious jewel in the vastness of space.

And heading straight toward it, a malevolent ball of dark fire.

"A little over an hour, sir!"


Father Cornelius and David went first, down the long passageway, into the underground chamber.

Korben followed, carrying Leeloo in his arms.

Loc Rhod came last with the stones.

By the time Korben got to the central chamber, David and Cornelius had already lighted the ceremonial room with strategically placed balls of sputtering light.

Crude and smoky, but effective.

There was an altar at the center of the chamber.

Korben laid Leeloo on it, gently.

Reverently, even.

Around the altar were four stone pedestals. Father Cornelius was going from one to the other, examining them.

"This one must be . . . water," he said uncertainly.

Korben was suspicious. "Don't tell me you don't know how it works!"

"Of course I do!" Father Cornelius said. "Theoretically, anyway. The four stones are placed around the altar, and the Fifth Element is there, in the middle."

He nodded toward the altar, where Leeloo was sleeping peacefully. "If we set it up right, the weapon against Evil should work."

"But you've never *seen* it work," Korben said.

Cornelius shrugged. "Uh, thank God . . . no!"

Korben, always the man of action, took one of the stones from the shirt Loc Rhod held in his arms, like a lumpy baby.

"OK, let's see. Every weapon has a manual. It's got to be around here somewhere."

He held the stone up in the dim, smoky light, examining the symbol carved on it.

Air.

He carried it to one of the four pedestals, also carved with a symbol.

Air.

A match.

"Let's do it!" said Korben. "Match the symbols."

Father Cornelius, David and Loc Rhod took the remaining three stones, and after a few mixups, matched them to their proper bases.

Then they all stood back, watching to see what would happen.

Waiting for something to happen.

Waiting for anything to happen.

"Nothing's happening," said Korben. "It doesn't work!"

"Of course not, not yet," said Father Cornelius. "The Stones have to be open."

"Open? You know how to do that?"

"Theoretically . . ." said Father Cornelius. "Theoretically . . . no."

On the other side of the small, threatened globe known as Earth, the President of the United Federation was in his office, watching the remote feed on the wall-sized viewscreen.

It showed a dark planet heading straight for Earth at blinding speed.

"Leeloo!"

Korben was bending over her, trying to awaken her.

"The Stones! Do you know how to open them?"

Korben had to bend way over to listen. With his hand behind his back, he motioned for his companions to be still.

Leeloo's voice was as soft as the single string of a harp.

"The wind blows . . . the fire burns . . ."

"I know all that, Leeloo!" Korben said. "But what about the Stones?!"

". . . rain falls . . ."

"Let her rest," said Father Cornelius. "It's the only way for her to heal."

Korben backed away, frustrated.

He picked up one of the stones off its pedestal. "The rain falls . . . the wind blows . . . what the hell does that mean?"

"Maybe it's a game!!" Loc Rhod offered. "Like charades??"

"No!" Korben said, replacing the Stone in its pedestal. "It's much simpler. If we don't figure out how these things open in five minutes, we're all dead. Got it?"

"Got it!!" said Loc Rhod.


The evil planet drew closer and closer. Instead of light, it threw off darkness. Its shadow preceeded it, slicing across the blue planet like an eclipse.

On the desert, a darkness fell over the sand, cooling it instantly.

Inside the temple, the blue globes sputtered and went out.

In the President's office, a tech turned a worried face away from the communications console.

"We've lost contact with Cornelius and Dallas."

"How much time?" asked the President.

"Three minutes."

☼     ☼     ☼

"We'll never make it!!" said Loc Rhod.

He was holding a flashlight, while Cornelius, David and Korben tried each stone in turn, shaking them, turning them, knocking them together—all to no avail.

Loc Rhod bent over one the stones and let out a hopeless sigh . . .

*Pop!*

Korben, David and Cornelius all wheeled around at the slight popping sound.

Loc Rhod picked up the stone. "It moved!! Korben!! Korben!!"

Korben, Cornelius and David rushed over. The stone seemed to be swelling slightly.

"What did you do?" asked Korben. "What did you say?"

"Nothing!! Swear to god, I didn't do nothing!!"

Korben grabbed the DJ by one ultra-padded shoulder. "Look, you did *something* that set it off. Try to remember. Concentrate. Tell me exactly what you did!"

Loc Rhod bent over the pedestal. "I was like this, with my hands here, and I said 'we'll never make it'!! That's all!!"

"And then?" asked Father Cornelius.

"And then?" asked David.

"And then?" asked Korben

"And then I guess I sighed. Like this."

Loc Rhod sighed.

*Pop pop!*

The stone opened even more.

"I've got it!" said Korben. "The wind! The wind blows . . ."

He bent over and blew gently on the Sacred Stone.

A small square opened, showing a bright blue patch of sky, complete with miniature clouds. A yellow beam of light shone up, illuminating the wide smile on Korben's rugged face.

"Everyone on a Stone!" he yelled. "Water for water! Fire for fire! Earth for Earth!"

David scraped up a handful of dust and tossed it on his stone.

*Pop pop pop!*

A patch of green appeared, and a green beam lighted his eager young face.

Father Cornelius looked around for water— then mopped his brow with a handkerchief, and wrung a few drops of sweat onto his stone.

*Pop pop pop!*

A tiny window opened, revealing a raging sea, complete with whitecapped waves. A blue beam of light shone up on the old priest's face.

Loc Rhod was having trouble with the fourth stone.

He was going through his pockets. (There were lots of them.)

"I don't have a light!!" he said. "I quit smoking last week!!"

Korben patted his own pockets, and found his box of matches.

There was one left.

"Don't breathe!" he said.

He struck the match.

A tiny flame appeared . . .

sputtered . . .

flickered . . .

Dead silence gripped the room as Korben approached the stone with the tiny flickering match.

Loc Rhod, David and Father Cornelius stood stock still, like statues.

Leeloo lay languidly on the altar.

Cupping the tiny flame in his ham-sized hand, Korben tiptoed toward the fourth stone.

He touched the flame to the stone.

*Pop pop pop!*

A patch of fire appeared within the stone, and a bright red beam flashed out, joining the yellow, the green and the blue beams on the ceiling of the temple.


"How much time?" asked the President.

His eyes were fixed on the viewscreen, which was filled with the nightmare vision of the approaching ball of dark fire.

"One minute."


"Leeloo!" said Korben.

He centered her on the altar, where the four beams criss-crossed.

"Let's go!" he said. "According to Father Cornelius, it's your move . . ."

In the shadows, the old priest and his novice were praying softly.

Loc Rhod was standing beside them, muttering his own form of prayer.

Leeloo rose to her knees.

"Protect life . . ." she said. "Until death . . ."

Her eyes closed.

"You can sleep tomorrow!" said Korben, shaking her gently. "Come on . . ."

"I want . . . to sleep . . . forever. . . ."

"No!" said Korben, shaking her harder. "You can't! The world needs you—and I need you, too. I'll take you on a vacation afterwards. A real vacation this time, for as long as you like! Come on! Wake up, baby! Time to work!"

Korben stepped back as Leeloo struggled to her feet in the intersection of the four beams.

She stood, wavering unsteadily, and a white beam of light formed around her, shining straight up toward the ceiling of the temple.

"Come on, Leeloo!" said Cornelius.

"Come on!" said David.

"Green!!" said Loc Rhod.

The white beam, rose—

Then weakened and grew dim, as Leeloo fell to her knees on the altar—

Then collapsed to the floor.


The dark planet filled the viewscreen.

The President wanted to close his eyes, but he couldn't.

He had been a boxer at Annapolis, and he knew the feeling.

It was too familiar. It was when you were losing, waiting, watching the knock-out punch coming straight at you.

In slow motion.

"Fifty seconds," said the tech.


"Leeloo!"

Korben picked her up off the floor.

The walls behind him were oozing a mysterious black liquid.

It squeezed from the stone walls and fell in hideous drops, like something from the grave.

It dropped its splatters onto the floor, hissing ominously where it hit.

One drop fell at Loc Rhod's feet and ate a hole in the stone floor.

*SSSsssssss!*

Loc Rhod backed away, barely dodging another drop. And another.

Whatever it was, it was falling like rain. A final deadly acid rain.


"Leeloo!"

Korben helped her back onto the altar, into the light of the crossed beams.

He climbed onto the altar with her. He stood with her, helping her to her feet.

"If you don't get with the program, we're all going to die!" he whispered into her ear. "And that's not on my schedule for today!"

Leeloo wrapped her arms around his neck and hung there, exhausted.

"What's the use?" she whispered. "What's the use of saving lives, when you see what you humans do with them?"

"You're right!" said Korben. "But there are lots of good things. Beautiful things worth saving."

"Like . . ."

"Love, for example!"

"But I don't . . . know love. So there is no need for me, other than this . . ."

"Wrong!" said Korben. "The world needs you. But I need you even more. More than you can imagine. Stand up straight!"

"Why?" Leeloo looked straight up into Korben's worried, tormented face. "Why would you . . . need me?"

"Because . . ." said Korben.


"Tell her!" muttered Cornelius to himself. "Tell her, for God's sake!"

He was pressed against the wall with David.

A drop of black fire dropped on Loc Rhod's shirt.

*SSSsssss!*

He ripped off the shirt and threw it away.

"Tell her!" muttered Father Cornelius.

☼    ☼    ☼

"Because!" said Korben again.

Leeloo looked up at Korben.

Her eyes were like twin green earths, filled with tears like shining seas.

"Tell me," she said.

"Because I love you," said Korben.

Leeloo smiled shyly. "Now you have permission."

"Permission?"

"To kiss me."

And Korben did.

And the white beam grew brighter around them.

The Divine Light grew in intensity until it filled the temple and burst through the top, scattering sand (and a stray camel or two) like an explosion as it soared upward, into the upper reaches of the atmosphere, where it struck the ball of dark fire just as it was beginning to enter the atmosphere . . .


In the temple, Korben and Leeloo kissed like there was no tomorrow.

Only, there was.

Thanks to them, there would be many tomorrows.

The black liquid oozing from the walls solidified into stalactites that broke off and shattered on the floor of the temple.

The dark planet *screeched* with a sound like screams. And began to harden and crust over. . . .

In the office of the President, two massive eyes opened under a broad brow.

The President realized that he was still alive. And so was the planet Earth.

"The intruder seems to have stopped, sir," said the tech. "Sixty-two miles from impact! It has fallen into a harmless orbit."

The President breathed out, and as he did he realized he hadn't breathed in for several minutes.

Breathing felt wonderfully, miraculously good.

Lindberg even smiled.

The white beam had lost its intensity, but Korben and Leeloo were still standing, washed in the flickering of light that lapped around them like the gentle waves of a receding ebb tide.

It was a long kiss.

Father Cornelius and David were on their knees, just finishing their prayers.

Loc Rhod opened his eyes.

"This guy's a killer with the babes," he confided to Father Cornelius. "I knew it from the moment I laid eyes on him."

Cornelius and David laughed.

Leeloo and Korben kept on kissing.

# 29

**"MR. PRESIDENT!"**

The door to the Neurological Lab burst open, and in came President Lindberg, followed by his retinue of aides, techs, scientists and military advisers—all in bright ceremonial dress.

Professor Mactilburgh stepped forward, bowing graciously to his guests.

"Mr. President," an aide announced. "Allow me to introduce Professor Mactilburgh, who runs the center."

"It's an honor to receive you, Mr. President," intoned Mactilburgh.

The President's eyes were already darting around the lab. "Where are our two heroes?"

"They were so tired from their ordeal," said Mactilburgh, "that we put them in the reactor this morning, so that . . ."

Lindberg cut him short with a wave of the Presidential hand. "I have nineteen meetings after this one, professor."

Mactilburgh knew when he was being told to get on with it. "Let me go see if they've revived."

"We go live in one minute, Mr. President," whispered another aide.

Mactilburgh pressed a button on the side of the reactor chamber, which made its blue shield translucent.

Inside, Korben and Leeloo were entwined in one another's arms, kissing.

They were naked.

"I, uh, think they need a little more time, Mr. President," said Mactilburgh.

The President nodded. Hearing a nearby commotion, he looked over to still another aide, who was holding a cell phone nervously.

"No, ma'am!" the aide said. "I tried. I know! No, ma'am!"

"Who is it?" the President asked.

The aide covered the phone. "Some woman who claims she's Major Dallas's mother."

"Give it here."

The President took the phone.

"Mrs. Dallas, this is the President. On behalf of the entire Federation, I would like to thank . . ."

The President frowned and held the phone away from his ear.

The entire lab turned toward him—and heard a shrill, tiny, tinny voice:

"Don't pull that crap on me, Finger. I'd recognize that trash can voice of yours in a dark alley during a rainstorm. You tell that worthless no account son of mine that he should plotz for the way he's ignored his mother. When I think of all I sacrificed for him!"

The President let the phone dangle from his fingers, like a dead fish.

"Mr. President . . ."

He turned and looked out the window. Something was happening to the east.

Behind him, Korben and Leeloo were bathed in the blue light of the chamber, still wrapped in their eternal (or so it seemed) kiss.

Outside, to the east, the skyline glowed with pale silvery light. The President smiled. It was one of his favorite sights.

Moonrise over Manhattan.

First the old moon, then the new one.